SNOOPING STABLEBOYS

M'LADY LUGGERTUCK

CONSTABLE WHOLECLOTH

NEVERPSLY V. LOAFBURTON

SIR FALSTAFF

COL. SITWELL

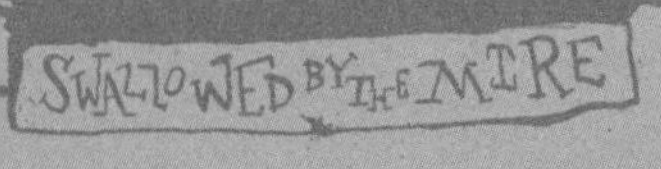
SWALLOWED BY THE MIRE

BUMP IN THE DARK

NAPOLEON

LORD EMBERLY

HILLHEMP, HOGBAG, GATEBERRY

OLD BART

THE DISHES

SIEGFRIED

BLIGHT + BLEMISH

LUTHER AND MONTGOMERY

SIR LUGGERTUCK

THE LUMP

CELIA

SMUGWICK MANOR

MONSIEUR P SMÉZAP

THE PERFUMING

HORTON

THE ABDUCTION!!

PORTNOY SLEEPS

OLD CROTTY

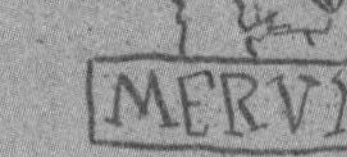
MERVIN

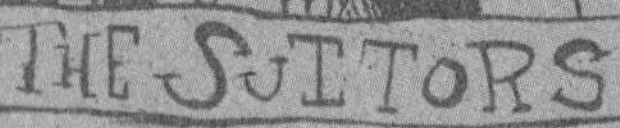
THE SUITORS

HORTON HALFPOTT
THE FIENDISH MYSTERY OF SMUGWICK MANOR
OR
THE LOOSENING OF M'LADY LUGGERTUCK'S CORSET
OR

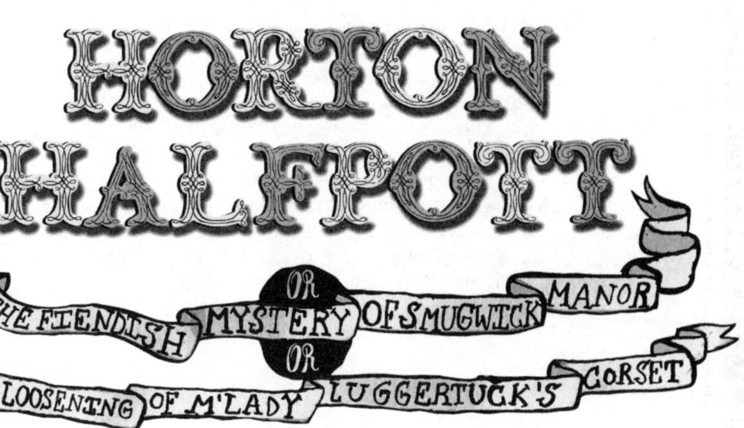

Tom Angleberger

With illustrations by the author

Amulet Books
New York

PUBLISHER'S NOTE: This is a work of fiction. Names, characters, places, and incidents are either the product of the author's imagination or are used fictitiously, and any resemblance to actual persons, living or dead, business establishments, events, or locales is entirely coincidental.

Library of Congress Cataloging-in-Publication Data

Angleberger, Tom.
Horton Halfpott, or, The fiendish mystery of Smugwick Manor, or, The loosening of M'Lady Luggertuck's corset / Tom Angleberger.
p. cm.
ISBN 978-0-8109-9715-8 (alk. paper)
[1. Household employees—Fiction. 2. Social classes—Fiction. 3. Conduct of life—Fiction. 4. Eccentrics and eccentricities—Fiction. 5. Great Britain—History—Victoria, 1837-1901—Fiction. 6. Mystery and detective stories.] I. Title. II. Title: Fiendish mystery of Smugwick Manor. III. Title: Loosening of M'Lady Luggertuck's corset.
PZ7.A585Hor 2011
[Fic]—dc22
2010038096

Book design by Melissa Arnst

Printed and bound in U.S.A.
10 9 8 7 6 5 4 3 2 1

ABRAMS
THE ART OF BOOKS SINCE 1949
115 West 18th Street
New York, NY 10011
www.abramsbooks.com

This book is dedicated to
John Christopher, with my
thanks for *The White Mountains*
and his many other wonderful
books, which have fascinated,
challenged, and amazed me.

MAP of SMUGWICK

MANOR & ENVIRONS

The Cast of

Luggertucks & Guests

The Heiress

The Press

Characters

Servants

Cops & Robbers

1

In Which the Corset Is Loosened . . .

There are so many exciting things in this book—a Stolen Diamond, snooping stable boys, a famous detective, the disappearance of a Valuable Wig, love, pickle éclairs, unbridled Evil, and the Black Deeds of the Shipless Pirates—that it really does seem a shame to begin with ladies' underwear.

But the underwear, you see, is the reason that all those Unprecedented Marvels happened—with the possible exception of the pickle éclairs. The underwear in question was a painful item called a corset. A corset, you see, is a sort of undershirt made of straps and sticks and strings and whalebones. In the days of horse-drawn carriages and powdered wigs, some women—and some men—would strap themselves into a corset and it would squeeze them and pinch them so much that they would look skinny.

Imagine being pinched like that day after day, year after year. It could make a nice lady into a mean one. So imagine what it would do to a lady like M'Lady Luggertuck, who was a nasty beast to start.

Our story begins one morning, long after the corset had turned M'Lady Luggertuck into one of the worst people in the world. For some reason, which no one knows, M'Lady Luggertuck decided not to be pinched and squeezed that morning.

"Not quite so tight today, Crotty," said M'Lady Luggertuck as Old Crotty, her lady's maid, pulled at her corset strings.

Old Crotty gasped. And she was not the sort who gasps very often. In fact, it had been seventeen years since she had expressed surprise of any kind.

But in Old Crotty's long memory there had never been a day when M'Lady Luggertuck had not wanted her corset as tight as Crotty could get it. Crotty was a tiny old thing, but she could pull those corset strings tighter than a hangman's noose. But not this day. A disappointed Crotty gave the strings not the usual mighty yank, but only a halfhearted tug.

"Ah, that feels much better, Crotty," said M'Lady Luggertuck.

What with the rest of the dressing and a trip to the westernmost linen closet, a full twenty minutes elapsed before Old Crotty arrived in the kitchen to supervise the twisting of the customary Luggertuck Breakfast Fruitbraid.

And yet, in those twenty minutes, did it not seem that the news of the Unprecedented Marvel of the Loosened Corset had already spread throughout Smugwick Manor? Did it not seem to have already disturbed the stagnant air of the place from root cellar to turret?

There was a feeling amongst the servants that they might get away with, say, wiping their noses on their sleeves—an offense that would normally cost them their job. Footmen felt they might slouch a little. Maids felt they might scrub less thoroughly.

And in the kitchen . . . the iron rule of law was felt to be just a little rusty.

When Crotty finally reached the kitchen, she found no cook preparing to braid the Luggertuck Breakfast Fruitbraid. Another shock to the old maid.

The reason for the cook's absence was Horton Halfpott, the lowest, most pathetic kitchen boy in the whole place. The cook, Miss Neversly, had found it necessary to beat him—yet again.

Horton had dropped a stack of firewood somewhat carelessly next to the stove. That sort of thing was not done! The firewood was to be placed by the stove one piece at a time, very carefully and very quietly. When the pulpy clank of the dropped wood rang out, the cook had abandoned the Fruitbraid in favor of cracking young Halfpott on the head with a wooden spoon, repeatedly.

"Lazy, lazy, lazy boy!" roared Miss Neversly, a middle-aged woman with two hundred years' worth of meanness in her. Her wild black hair whipped across her furious face as she swung her spoon at the kitchen boy. "Wretched wart-covered ape!"

Beware, Reader; do not form an opinion of Horton based on Miss Neversly's cruel words. True, he had just been a trifle careless in the matter of firewood fetching. However, he is to be the hero of our story and it is only fair to point out that he was ill-paid and ill-treated for his services, which mostly involved the washing of dishes and were normally done quite carefully.

Also, please don't judge him by his appearance. His clothes were grubby because he only had one set and he worked in a messy kitchen. His brown hair was messy because he didn't have a comb or a brush. His head was a little wobbly, his nose was kind of funny, and his lips were a little too lippy because that's just the way they were.

He was a smart boy and a pretty friendly one, too, but those qualities rarely shine when you're stuck in a hot, smoky, greasy kitchen day after day after day.

"Please stop hitting me with your spoon, Miss Neversly," Horton said. See, Reader? He was polite and mannerly, even in those circumstances, even while being beaten about the head with a wooden spoon.

"How many times have I told you not to drop the firewood?" demanded Neversly.

"Why, never, Miss Neversly. You've never had occasion to tell me, because this is the first time I've ever done it."

This was quite true. He had of course wanted to drop the firewood, as any kitchen boy would. Kitchen boys do not see the merits of bending down and gently placing firewood on the floor. And rightly so—it's bad for the back.

Nonetheless, Horton Halfpott had never dropped the firewood before. Here, in Smugwick Manor, the ancestral home of the Luggertucks, there had always been a sense that such behavior simply wasn't proper.

But today things were different. There had been a Loosening. Horton felt it, and so did everyone else. And may God have mercy on their souls!

In Which Evil Wakes Earlier Than Usual . . .

The Loosening was felt from manor to lodge, arbor to alcove, garden to gable.

The strict rules that had long governed Smugwick Manor, the rules that kept servants obedient and M'Lady Luggertuck omnipotent, had been relaxed. Not done away with, mind you, but relaxed just a tiny little bit, which is more than they'd ever been relaxed before.

The servants weren't the only ones to feel it.

Deep in the bowels of the manor, an Ancient Evil stirred to life.

Actually, it wasn't all that ancient—only about sixteen years old. But it was Evil, all right. And its name was . . . Luther Luggertuck.

Luther, the offspring of M'Lady and Sir Whimperton Luggertuck and the heir to Smugwick Manor, normally slept late. But that morning the Loosening tugged him from his wicked, wicked dreams.

He felt the change, and it frightened him. He liked things Tight, not Loose. He liked being able to boss people around and treat them like dirt. It was his birthright.

He slithered from his room and went to see what was going on.

Peering around a corner, he saw Old Crotty whispering with Footman Jennings, who was also old but didn't like being called Old Jennings. They appeared to be flirting! Disgusting! Servants aren't supposed to enjoy themselves.

Putting his ear to a door, he eavesdropped upon Colonel Osgood Sitwell, a permanent houseguest at Smugwick Manor. Luther was shocked to hear the Colonel say thank you to Milly, the new maid.

Disgraceful! Gentlemen didn't thank servants, they ordered them about!

While hiding behind a bush, Luther saw his father taking a stroll in the garden with a slight smile upon his face. Unbelievable! He didn't even know his father could do such a thing with his lips.

Sneaking in a back door, he came across Horton Halfpott carrying a tray piled with freshly washed silverware. The filthy boy was humming! No one hums in Smugwick Manor!

Luther tripped Horton and the silverware went flying. Normally Horton would have been prepared to dodge Luther's kicks and shoves, but he hadn't expected him to be up so early.

"Very sorry, Master Luggertuck," said Horton, because that is how a servant is expected to respond to the Heir of Smugwick's mistreatment.

"Pick it all up and rewash it!" ordered Luther. "I'll be checking it at lunchtime! If I find a speck of dirt, I'll have you whipped."

"Of course, Master Luggertuck," said Horton, already thinking of Miss Neversly's reaction to his returning to the kitchen with dirty silverware. And he'd be in even worse trouble if he tried to blame Luther.

Long before Horton had picked up the last of the spilled spoons, Luther had wound his way to the other side of the castle where lay M'Lady's Chambers.

Moving aside a painting, *Two Dogs Eating a Dead Gopher*, Luther put his eye to a secret peephole and spied on M'Lady herself. This was a thing he rarely dared to do. For one thing, he didn't want to see M'Lady in her underwear and, for another, M'Lady was the one mortal who frightened him. She was a Considerably Larger and Somewhat More Ancient Evil.

But all of the Unprecedented Marvels he had just seen had Luther rattled. He didn't know about the corset, of course, but he was certain his mother must have something to do with the Loosening, since, after all, she was the one who normally kept things Tight.

Ah, Luther, you scoundrel, if only you knew—the Loosening was just the beginning.

Another preternatural force had been unleashed, and it was at that moment a'hurtling down upon Smugwick Manor like a summer thunderstorm. A force stronger than any other, with the power to fell a man in an instant.

Love—yes, Love—was about to buffet the weathered stone of the manor, whose musty corridors had gone many fine years without it.

It is the collision of these forces that interests us, Reader. For without the Loosening, Love would have found no foothold among the Luggertucks and would have winged its way onward.

But Love, which had taken the earthly form of a letter to M'Lady Luggertuck, did find a place to land that day. And that letter also opened the way for robbery, rudeness, treachery, and Shipless Piracy. (It is my opinion that the Pickle Éclair Disaster would have happened either way.)

Luckily for Luther—and the plot of this story—M'Lady read the letter aloud as she sat in her Letter-Writing Nook.

> *Dearest sister,* ["HA!" M'Lady said with a snort.]
>
> *I ask, for young Montgomery's sake, that you put the unfortunate incident of last Christmas behind you.* ["HARRUMPH!" barked M'Lady as she recalled the terrible events that readers will

remember from "M'Lady Luggertuck and the Yule Log."]

Whatever feelings you hold toward me need not, I hope, prevent you from bestowing your well-known and frequently commented-upon generosity of spirit on my son, your nephew, Montgomery.

Montgomery informs us that he is in love. The object being a Miss Celia Sylvan-Smythe.

Miss Sylvan-Smythe is spending the summer with your neighbors, the Shortleys.

Might not Montgomery stay with you for a few weeks to increase his proximity to the young girl and thus also his chances of seeing the sweet blossoms of romance bloom? And perhaps most important, might you not throw a ball that the young girl be invited to?

["HMMMMM," murmured M'Lady.]

Signed,

Your beloved sister,

Duchess Carolyn Crimcramper

Now, M'Lady Luggertuck had often been asked to give balls before, for this or that niece, nephew, or illegitimate stepson. But as readers of "M'Lady

Luggertuck Tries a Waltz" well know, such requests were usually crumpled up and stomped on.

But this letter was not. This letter was met with a "hmmmmm."

Why? The Loosened Corset, of course.

Normally, when M'Lady sat in her cramped Writing Nook, her corset pinched painfully, making her grumpy and rude when she wrote her responses. But today there was no pinch and her response was nearly cheerful.

"Yes," she replied—as Luther looked on in surprise—"yes, send the boy down, he shall have his ball, and the young lady, Miss Sylvan-Smythe, shall be the guest of honor."

And thus she sealed their doom.

3

In Which the Purple Bell Rings . . .

Before doom descends on Smugwick Manor, let us take a moment to look around the place.

'Twas topped with glittering spires and turrets, true. But 'twas bottomed with dank, moldy basements, cellars, vaults, crypts, plant-pressing rooms, and tunnels.

The areas in between the top turrets and bottom basements were old and worn and well-polished by servants.

Life at Smugwick Manor was very, very, very nice. Nice, that is, if one was a Luggertuck; otherwise it was very, very, very not nice.

Since there were only a few Luggertucks, but scores of footmen, maids, kitchen hands, stable boys, gardeners, polishers, and other attendants, most of the people at Smugwick Manor were living the not-nice part. (Alas, Milly, the new maid, was still blissfully unaware of just how not nice things normally were.)

A few of the older servants remembered what it was like before Sir Luggertuck married M'Lady. His father, kindly Old Lord Emberly Luggertuck, had been generous with his money and stingy only with complaints.

M'Lady Luggertuck was just the opposite.

When she finally drove Old Lord Emberly out of the manor and into the rundown assistant gamekeeper's cottage in the woods, she took over the running of the household. She cut the pay of every servant in half. Then, a year later, in half again. And so on.

Whilst shopping for wigs or frilled garments, M'Lady Luggertuck demanded the best. (See "M'Lady Luggertuck and the Unlucky Cobbler.") But when she doled out the money for the servants' food each month, Reader, she demanded the least!

"Which gruel is the cheapest?" she asked the cook,

Miss Neversly. "Are you certain you're adding enough water?"

Once, she learned that each garden boy received bread crusts and water.

"Really, does a garden boy need bread *crusts*, plural?" she said with a sniff. "Shouldn't bread *crust*, singular, do just as well?"

And Woe—yes, Woe—to any servant caught pinching a bit of food from the kitchen.

Even scraps left over from the Luggertucks' feasts were off-limits. These were the sole property of Sir Luggertuck's Foxhounds and certainly not for any kitchen boy to go a'grabbing.

Miss Neversly had trained her ears to catch the slightest sound of food felony. The chewing of a raisin she could hear. The swallowing of a bit of gristle sounded to her like an alarm bell. The licking of a finger rang in her ears from two rooms away.

Punishment for any of these offenses, and many others, included a sound beating with her wooden spoon and the loss of a week's wages.

Thus it was that servants, hungry and generally angry, waited every week for the ringing of the purple bell.

You see, the lives of servants are not lived by clocks, but by the ringing of their masters' bells.

Throughout Smugwick Manor hung little silver ropes with golden tassels. If a Luggertuck wanted anything at all at any time at all, they had but to tug on the nearest little silver rope. Down in the kitchen one of many color-coded bells would ring, and the servants would know in which room a Luggertuck was waiting impatiently.

Old Crotty and Miss Neversly knew by heart the sound of every bell.

Except one.

They'd never in their lives heard the purple bell. They would not have known what it meant even if they heard it. They didn't even know which room held the little silver rope that made it ring.

And I personally hope they never find out.

You see, each week Old Crotty and Miss Neversly would go into town to buy the succulent foodstuffs that the Luggertucks feasted upon, as well as the single bag of stale gruel that the servants ate. Off they would go in a little donkey cart—the crazed raven-haired cook with the shopping list and the timid gray-haired maid with the money purse.

On this day, the day of the Loosening, the stable boys lined up to watch them go with even more excitement than usual.

As soon as they were out of sight, Bump, the smallest stable boy, ran into the third horse stall on the right, removed a board from the wall, reached into the wall behind it, and tugged with all his might on the little silver cord that was hidden there.

Every servant had spent the morning straining their ears for the bright, tinkling sound of the purple bell. When it came, they did not whoop and shout or even smile. They would not want to make M'Lady Luggertuck suspicious.

But deep, deep inside they rejoiced. The cook and housekeeper were gone. The time had come to eat.

Slowly, sneakily, they made their way to the kitchens, far beneath M'Lady's rooms and—more to the point—well out of earshot.

"Welcome, Bump!" called Loafburton, the burly Hungarian baker. "Welcome, Footman Jennings. Welcome, Slugsalt and Ernestine and Rosehip and Wickleweaver!"

"Well met, Loafburton," they called. "What will we eat today?"

"Only gruel and bread crusts," cried Loafburton with a wink, pulling buns and tarts and pies and cakes from his oven.

The servants didn't waste their time complaining about how bad the Luggertucks were. Instead they laughed and danced and sang and ate like Luggertucks.

Once a week, for one hour, and one hour only, life for the servants was very, very, very nice. Except for one servant.

"Horton, come and have a piece of Sweet Sugar-apple Pie," Loafburton always said. He was a kindly man who often thought of Horton in a fatherly way.

"Hort, come on and have a rhubarb tart," said Bump, the small stable boy who was Horton's best friend.

Two other stable boys, Blight and Blemish, also called to Horton.

"Mr. Halfpott, might I suggest a slice of fudge pudding cake?" asked Blight, a large boy with a lumpy head.

"Perhaps Mr. Halfpott would prefer pudding cake fudge?" suggested Blemish, a lumpy boy with a large head.

(Since Blight and Blemish hoped someday to become butlers, they were always extraordinarily polite and a little bit too wordy.)

But no matter how they tried, they always received the same response:

"No, thank you," Horton said, busy at his sink, washing dishes.

4

In Which Halfpott History Is Revealed . . .

The ringing of the purple bell signaled Horton's least favorite time of the week. He would rather endure a spoon beating.

Horton simply could not bring himself to take a cake.

He would have liked one, of course. He was just as hungry as everyone else.

But Horton could not bring himself to break a rule. Even on a day such as that one, when there had been a Loosening, he could not break a rule.

Loafburton had almost given up trying.

“Skin and bones you are, my good Horton,” he said. “M’Lady Luggertuck doesn’t feed you enough to live on. You’ll drop over dead right in your sink one of these days.”

Horton knew that Loafburton was right. He knew that M’Lady Luggertuck was cruel and mean and wrong.

It made him angry at himself. It made him miserable. But it just seemed wrong to take the Luggertucks’ food.

Plus, he asked himself with horror, what if he lost his week’s wages or—much worse—his job at Smugwick Manor?

Ah yes, Reader, I know what you are thinking. You think that losing an awful job in an awful place for awful pay would be a good thing.

But Horton had a reason. His reason was the other Halfpotts—his mother, his brothers and sisters, old Uncle Lemuel, and his father, who had been sick for so long.

Every Sunday morning—the only free time allotted to the Luggertucks’ servants—Horton ran down the road, through the village, across ten fields and three streams, to the cottage where his family lived.

He gave his mother the single copper penny he had earned. She smiled and put it in a little tin can.

"Now do we have enough to pay for a doctor?" Horton always asked.

"Almost, Horton, almost," she always said.

He had just enough time to shake hands with old Uncle Lemuel, to hug his little brothers and sisters, and to kneel down beside his father's sickbed, before he had to turn around and run back.

The Luggertucks' penny was a paltry thing, but it was all the money the Halfpotts had.

And so Horton was grateful and, yes, even faithful to the Luggertucks, who deserved it not at all.

4

Addendum

In Which the Stable Boys' History Is Not Revealed . . .

A word, please, about Bump, Blight, and Blemish before we move on.

From whence came they, you may ask. Were they orphans? Brothers? Royal princes hidden away to protect them from the scheming archduke who had seized control of the throne?

They did not know. They'd all been working in the Luggertuck stables as long as they could remember. Oddly, none of the older stable boys, nor even the stable master for that matter, could remember when they arrived.

A rumor among some of the ruder servants was that Blight and Blemish were twins who were given away by their parents because they were so ugly. While it is true that they had a certain toadlike appearance, I cannot imagine that their own mother would have thought them ugly.

As for Bump, there was a rumor that he was raised by wolves. I find that very hard to believe.

Bump had lots and lots of friends among the servants, but Horton was his very best friend.

Sometimes, after he finished his work in the stables—and, more important, after Miss Neversly had gone to bed—Bump sneaked into the kitchen and helped Horton wash the piles and piles of dirty dishes.

That's what he did the night of the Loosening.

"Hort! You'll never, ever, ever guess what I just saw," Bump chattered excitedly. "Old Crotty and Footman Jennings walking in the garden."

"What?" cried Horton.

"Yep, holding hands."

"There's many strange things going on today, Bump,"

said Horton, "but that's the best I've heard yet. He's been in love with her for years."

"What do you think will happen next?" asked Bump.

"Who knows," said Horton. "Maybe *you'll* fall in love."

"Me?" squeaked Bump. "Forget it. I bet it'll be you."

"Hmmph, not very likely," said Horton. And he didn't say anything else for a while.

What he said had been true and he knew it, and it made him sad. It wasn't very likely that he'd fall in love. In fact, nothing was very likely except that the next day he'd be in the kitchen again and the day after that and the day after that.

But Horton wasn't one to mope. It's true that he didn't have a lot of occasions to smile, but it was rare indeed to see him frown.

He turned his attention to making Bump laugh.

"Maybe Miss Neversly will be next," he said. "Maybe she'll fall in love."

What a thought! Mean old Miss Neversly in love. Why, that would be . . . an Unprecedented Marvel.

5

In Which Plans for Both the Costume Ball and Evil Deeds Are Made . . .

The next day, much to Old Crotty's surprise, M'Lady again asked for her corset to be "not so tight."

Thus the Loosening continued and everyone knew it. They didn't know the reason for it, but they sensed it and they liked it.

Except for Luther. He decided to do something about it. He decided to Whine.

Alas, Luther's Whining was not an Unprecedented Marvel. It was an everyday occurrence.

You see, Luther was not just Evil, he was also Annoying. You may blame M'Lady for both.

From the day of his birth, M'Lady had spoiled her son with excess, encouraged him when punishment was needed and, worst of all, taught him by example.

With such a mother, it is no wonder that Luther was a beastly baby, then a beastly boy, and now a beastly young gentleman.

"Motherrrrr," he whined, "about this ball . . ."

"Oh, isn't it exciting?" cooed M'Lady Luggertuck. Yes, she cooed. "It will be the grand event of the season. We'll be the envy of all society and I shall wear my newest Fashionable Wig!"

Luther was revolted by his mother's near-cheerfulness. He had been suckled on bitterness and bile and was quite disturbed to see her behaving in such a sunshiny fashion. He realized it was not to his advantage and did his best to call back the familiar storm clouds.

"What a stupid idea, Mother. What a waste of perfectly good money, feeding a lot of old ninnies and gassers, so they can stumble around our ballroom scuffing the floors and listening to an overpaid band of string pluckers."

"Oh, Luther, they won't all be old," said M'Lady Luggertuck, pawing at her son's starched collar. "Why, there are so many young ladies and gentlemen to invite that I've decided to make it a costume ball."

"Young ladies and gentlemen, Mother? Bah! Who? There is no one worth noticing within fifty leagues. Surely not the Reverend Apoplexy's dog-faced daughters? Not the Frimperton brothers?"

"Well, yes, of course they will be invited, but, just think, your cousin Montgomery will be there, as he is to spend the summer with us."

"Ugh!" groaned Luther.

"Ah, yes, dear Montgomery," M'Lady continued. "The poor young thing's in love. His mother has specifically asked us to invite the young lady he fancies, a Miss Sylvan-Smythe who is summering with the Shortleys. True love may blossom right here in fashionably decorated Smugwick Manor."

Longtime readers of M'Lady Luggertuck's adventures are no doubt surprised by just how mushy she can get without that corset tightening her heart (and, more important, her stomach). Here was a woman who married for money and hadn't spoken a kind word to her husband in years, and yet here she was babbling about romance. "True love! Just think of it, Luther!"

Luther thought, but not of true love. He thought of money.

The Luggertuck fortune was, as faithful readers well know, dwindling. Squandered. Frittered away. Spent on fashion and fad that fled the land long ago. (See "M'Lady Luggertuck's Parisian Shopping Spree.")

Oh, there was money enough for any decent family to live upon for generations. But the Luggertuck family had lost any slight claim it might have had to decency when M'Lady married into it.

Luther wanted more. Much more. And he certainly didn't plan to work for it. He planned, eventually, to marry for it.

He made it his business to know where money hung about, and a lot of it loitered in the Sylvan-Smythes' bank accounts.

Now he calculated the total wealth of the Sylvan-Smythes based on his knowledge of their land holdings, stock purchases, and investments in automated steam looms.

They were as rich as the Luggertucks had once been.

Luther hated to stop in the middle of a good Whine, but suddenly a ball sounded like quite a good idea. It would offer a chance to get close to the young lady. He would find a way to win Miss Sylvan-Smythe and, more important, the enormous dowry that came with her.

But wait, you ask, how could Luther—intolerable, obnoxious, odious, odoriferous, and generally unbearable—win the hand of the most sought-after young lady in England? Why, with an Evil Plan, of course.

And, like a fungus of the foot, just such a plan began to fester and grow in the damp recesses of Luther's brain—sporing from synapse to synapse until his whole head itched with it.

He now stood very much in favor of the ball, but felt he might still put his whine to good use. "Very well, Mother, but I shall need my allowance doubled to costume myself properly."

6

In Which Miss Neversly Is Disobeyed and Dawdling Occurs . . .

The next day, Old Crotty gathered the servants.

"M'Lady will throw a ball in two weeks' time, on the tenth of July. There is much work to do, but I know you are all as happy as I am to be able to help the Luggertucks shine on their special day."

No one, not even Footman Jennings, met her eye. No one was happy to help. No one cared whether the Luggertucks shone or not. They did care, however, about the two weeks of hard work that lay ahead in preparing for the ball.

Much of that work would fall to Horton, Bump, and the dozen or so other kitchen, stable, and garden boys. The chairs that had lurked in the east basement since the last Luggertuck ball would have to be toted one by one, the acreage of the ballroom waxed inch by inch, the miles of gravel lane from Smugwick Manor to the village raked foot by foot.

But their first task revealed itself as a pleasant one—the hand delivery of invitations to the homes of all those guests who lived within a day's walk. The footmen were supposed to do it, but they, being well aware that M'Lady's corset was still Loosened, chose instead to play cards in the pickle storeroom. The boys were more than happy to do the job, which they knew would give them ample opportunities to dawdle.

"Do not dawdle," Neversly ordered the boys, cracking Horton on the head with a spoon to make her point.

But dawdle they did.

It was the best day of the summer and they were loosed upon it.

Once out of Neversly's sight, they whooped, chased, wrestled, and tumbled.

Blight and Blemish, though not of athletic build, led the pack through Wolfleg Woods.

"Mr. Blemish, the proximity of Magpie Pond would appear to offer a pleasant refuge from the heat of the day," said Blight.

"Very good, Mr. Blight," said Blemish. "Shall we disrobe?"

Two enormous muddy splashes soon followed, as did the other boys.

"Come on, Horton, come on," called Bump, happily half out of his trousers.

"I can't, Bump, I'll never make it in time if I do," said Horton regretfully. He dodged Bump's attempts to push him in.

"Where are you bound, Mr. Halfpott?" called Blemish, bobbing in the middle of the rather murky pond. "I'm afraid I've drawn light duty today as I've only got to go to the minister's and Dr. Radish's."

"I've got to go all the way to the Shortleys'," replied Horton.

"By M'Lady Luggertuck's bustle!" cried Blemish.

"My good man, that's all the way across the county. Might I suggest that you cut through Simpkin's Mire if you want to make it there and back in a day. But I hasten to add, be vigilant for snakes."

"And wolves," added Blight.

"And quicksand," piped in Bump.

"Why am I always the unlucky one?" Horton moaned, then turned to trudge onward, ever onward with the sounds of his frolicking friends at his back.

Bump watched his friend go, and his little heart almost broke. He knew about Horton's family. He knew the reasons why Horton would never break the rules. But he hated to see Horton always missing out on the few things that made life at Smugwick almost bearable.

He ran toward the pond and leaped. In midair, he closed his eyes and wished for something wonderful to happen to Horton. And then he hit the cold water and went under, popping up a second later into the full glory of that perfect summer day.

Now, this isn't a fairy tale. And Bump's wish wasn't magic. But nevertheless, it was about to come true.

7

In Which Our Hero Falls into Two Things . . .

Horton did not understand his luck as he took the path to the edge of Simpkin's Mire, the giant swamp that covered half the county.

Nor did he understand his luck when he tripped and fell off the narrow path into the mosquitoed muck, emerging with one leg and one arm covered in stinking, putrid black mud.

However, hours later, he began to understand when, just moments after slogging out of the mire onto the

Shortleys' two-mile-long lane, he saw a very surprising thing—a girl on a bicycle.

Though a bicycle—a relatively new invention at that time—was a heretofore unseen sight this far from London, there was nothing particularly lucky about seeing it.

No, it is the rider of this clanky contraption that interests us. As she approached, Horton perceived her to be the most beautiful girl he had ever seen.

Not because of makeup or hairstyle, of which she seemed to have neither, but because of the smile she gave him. He had received few enough smiles in his life, and this was surely the best of the lot.

Fear not, Reader, we will not dwell on these romantic inklings, not if you don't wish to. But it really was a nice smile.

"Why, you're covered in mud," she called, wrestling with a lever in an attempt to brake the bicycle—a tall, ungainly structure with one big and one little wheel. It stopped suddenly and plopped her onto the ground. She laughed.

Horton ran over and offered her a hand. Unfortunately, black mud, smelling of dead tadpoles, still caked the aforesaid hand, as well as the rest of Horton's self.

“Er, no thanks,” she said. As she climbed to her feet, he realized she was twice as beautiful as he had first thought. But we don’t dwell; we move on.

“Sorry,” he mumbled, wiping his dirty hand on his dirty pants. “I fell in Simpkin’s Mire.”

“Is that the name of that swamp?” she asked. “What were you doing in there?”

“I had to come all the way from Smugwick Manor. I cut through the swamp to save time,” he said. “I’m delivering an invitation to the Shortleys.”

“Oh, really? I’ll be glad to take it the rest of the way for you.”

“Oh, do you work there?” he asked.

“No, I’m spending the summer there.”

A terrible feeling began to work its way through the Halfpott midsection and a terrible thought came to the Halfpott mind. This wasn’t a kitchen girl, as he had assumed because of her simple clothing. This wasn’t even a governess.

The girl gave a silly little mock curtsy.

“My name’s Celia Sylvan-Smythe. What’s yours?”

“Horton Halfpott, ma’am,” he said, and lowered his eyes respectfully.

This wasn't another servant, this was a young lady. A lady like M'Lady.

He had spoken to her. He had offered her a muddy hand. He had also entertained a certain notion that we're not dwelling on.

Humiliation set in fast. Certainly Miss Sylvan-Smythe did nothing to promote it. No, the humiliation came, as it so often does, of its own accord. It came of Horton's knowledge of the world—the way it worked and his place in it. He seemed unaware that Celia seemed unaware of the way the world worked and his place in it.

He yearned to go. The clammy, stinking mire seemed like a preferable place to be.

He held out the envelope. "Here, ma'am. The invitation."

She took it and laughed again. "You'll have to stop calling me ma'am if we're going to be friends. Besides, I'm only a miss."

He heard her, but he was already running. Back into the weeds, back through the muck to his proper place.

He had made a fool of himself, he realized, and worst of all, he would never have a chance to speak to her again.

8

In Which Horton's Competition Is Enumerated . . .

Such sad thoughts ran through our kitchen boy's head on the long slog back to Smugwick Manor.

But what of the lovely head of Celia Sylvan-Smythe? What thoughts ran through hers?

I shall not tell you, Reader. Miss Sylvan-Smythe is the only true lady in this story—even if she is just a girl—and I feel we owe her her privacy.

But I can tell you that she still had that nice smile when she picked up her bicycle and rode up the lane.

I can also tell you this.

Celia was too young to marry, but not to be engaged. Already, she had been wooed by no fewer than two dozen men. Stuffed shirts. Pompous popinjays. Greedy, as it were, pigs.

They were really wooing her father's money, and some didn't even try to hide this fact.

Oily, puffy, pasty, and dull, one and all. One was seventy-three years old. One was secretly already married. Most wore this year's fashions but had not read last year's books.

To say that they were slightly better than Luther Luggertuck is to say very little, and to say that Horton Halfpott was better than all of them put together is to state the obvious.

Word of the costume ball leaked out to these two dozen suitors and they quickly found ways to invite themselves.

But would their trip to Smugwick Manor be in vain? Was Celia's heart already taken? I can't say.

She leaned forward and whipped the bicycle up to top speed.

9

In Which Horton Is Rudely Received . . .

Horton arrived back at Smugwick Manor just after dark, stumbling up the drive in a state of muddiness, stinkiness, itchiness, and emotional confusion.

He expected to find the inhabitants of Smugwick Manor off to their nocturnal quarters—the Luggertucks to their stately bedchambers, the better servants to their small rooms, and his fellow lowly servants to their rickety cots in the stiflingly hot attic above the southeast wing, where it still smelled like pigeon dung although no pigeon had roosted there in forty years.

Instead, he found the manor alive. Lights bobbed behind windows as if candles were being carried from room to room. Several strange wagons sat in the drive, where all of the servants appeared to be assembled.

"Here, boy, what are you up to?" barked an extremely rude voice. It belonged to a rude man who grabbed Horton rudely around the neck.

"I—"

"What are you hiding, boy?" he demanded. (Rudely interrupting.)

"N—"

"Miss Neversly, is this filthy thing one of yours?" He dragged Horton toward the clump of servants. Even in the dim light, Horton's muddy clothes were plain to see. And his coating of mire mud stank by day or night.

Slugsalt, a garden boy, and some of his cronies laughed; Miss Neversly did not. Instinctively she grabbed for her spoon, but luckily for Horton's head she had left the spoon behind when she and the other kitchen staff were ordered outside.

"Yes, Constable Wholecloth," she said. "He's mine. One of my worst."

Then she turned on Horton. "Been lazing the day away in the pond, have you?"

"No, ma'am, I—"

"Or have you been sneaking about, hiding what you stole?"

"What? No, ma'am, I—"

"Someone fetch my spoon, I'll get the truth out of him!"

The baker, Loafburton, spoke up.

"Oh, Nell, leave him alone," he said.

Several servants gasped at his impudence and cowered as Miss Neversly's face turned red and her spoon hand twitched.

But the baker, a small man with strong, flour-covered arms, continued: "Don't you remember you sent him all the way to the Shortleys' today? He probably fell in the mire."

"Yes," cried Horton.

"Enough!" shrieked Miss Neversly. "Go to the stables and wash until the stink is gone. I won't have you tracking mud into my kitchen and you have many dishes to wash tonight."

“Wait!” barked Constable Wholecloth, coming toward Horton with a lantern. Horton could now see that the man indeed wore a policeman’s uniform a’dangling with badges, medals, epaulets, and sashes.

“Turn out your pockets,” the uniform said.

Horton did. They were empty except for a short candle stub. The constable, holding his nose, gave Horton a kick and told him to go wash.

Bump slipped away from the others and went with him. “You’ll never believe it, Hort!” he said.

“What on earth is going on?”

“Someone’s stolen the Lump!”

10

In Which We Learn of the Luggertuck Lump . . .

Some families have beautiful jewels that are passed down from generation to generation and are taken out only to wear at coronations, jubilees, and beheadings.

Some are pearl necklaces, others emerald brooches. There are golden rings and silver lockets and ruby tiaras.

The Luggertucks had a lump.

Except it was not just a lump, it was *the* Lump. The

Luggertuck Lump. Possibly the world's largest diamond and certainly the ugliest.

It was said that Sir Falstaff Luggertuck brought the Lump back with him from the Crusades. It did indeed look sort of like a diamond, but also a little like a rotten potato. It was said that the stone was so valuable that no jeweler dared to try making it look less like a potato, for fear of destroying nature's finest gift.

It was also said—but only in the servants' quarters and only in whispers—that the Lump was just a lump. It was ugly, it couldn't be worn, and it looked like any other rock.

Slugsalt said he pulled rocks like that out of the cabbage rows every day. However, it must be noted that Slugsalt had never actually seen the Lump.

Nevertheless, the Lump was the great treasure of the Luggertucks.

Along with Smugwick Manor, it was the only proof left that the Luggertucks were any better than the bankers, sea captains, tea merchants, and factory owners who now crowded the private clubs and fancy balls. Those people may have had money, but the

Luggertucks had nobility, class, royal blood, and the Lump.

Except they didn't have the Lump anymore. The lavish Lump Room, with its massive locks and solid marble pedestal, was found empty by Crotty herself.

Can it be any wonder, then, that M'Lady Luggertuck was heard to cry, "Send for Portnoy St. Pomfrey, the Greatest Detective in all of England!"

11

In Which the Great Detective Arrives . . .

The next day, four white stallions wearing feathery plumes on their heads pulled an enormous carriage up the drive.

To say that the inhabitants of Smugwick Manor had never seen a carriage like it would be to suggest that there was another carriage like it that they had simply not seen. There was not and still is not.

When Portnoy St. Pomfrey solved the Case of the Sultan's Sapphire, the sultan kindly offered to reward

St. Pomfrey with anything he wished. St. Pomfrey asked for the hand of the sultan's daughter in marriage.

When the sultan pointed out that his daughter was already married with three children, St. Pomfrey said he would settle for the "magnificent carriage" parked behind the sultan's palace instead.

The sultan was too polite to tell St. Pomfrey that this was really the Royal Outhouse. Instead, he ordered the outhouse set on wheels and shipped to England. St. Pomfrey has ridden in it ever since, always wondering about the lingering odor and lack of windows.

This wheeled water closet was immediately followed by another vehicle, one that was certainly a carriage, but a really lousy one. Out of this vehicle jumped three members of the press.

"M. Hillhemp of the *East London Tribune and Rannygazoo*," shouted the first as he leapt from the still-moving carriage.

"L. Gateberry of the *Wapping Worrier*," shouted the next, a young woman who hopped gracefully to the ground despite her long dress and petticoats.

"I. Howbag of the *West London Rannygazoo and Tribune*," hollered the last, tripping on the carriage steps and landing in a heap from which he sprang gymnastically, pulling a pad and pen from a pocket.

To whom these introductions were aimed remains unclear, as only Blight and Blemish happened to be near enough to the drive to bear witness to their arrival.

Hillhemp, Gateberry, and Howbag ran to the as-yet-unopened door of St. Pomfrey's carriage.

"Any leads on the Lump, sir?" called either Gateberry or Howbag.

"Is Sir Luggertuck's nephew Lord Crimcramper a suspect?" called another, who may have been Howbag, which means that the first one was Gateberry. Or Hillhemp.

Frankly, Reader, it is too difficult to tell these pen-brandishing members of the reporting trade apart. Their actions were so similar that I shall no longer bother.

It was their job to follow England's most famous detective and recount the details of his investigations in the pages of their newspapers. Do not judge them harshly. I worked among their number once. Their job was not easy.

The door of the carriage and the door of Smugwick Manor burst open at the same moment. From Smugwick

Manor came a stream of footmen, a valet, Crotty and, yes, M'Lady Luggertuck herself.

She was not surprised by the sight of the carriage, of course, having closely followed St. Pomfrey's adventures in the papers.

From the carriage came a commanding voice. Yes, it must be the great man himself! It must be Portnoy St. Pomfrey!

"Back! Get back you nattering nimrods of news, you journalistic jugwumps, you itchy inkers of inaccuracies!"

Hillhemp, Gateberry, and Howbag did not get back. They kept babbling questions.

A giant shoe emerged from the carriage. It was a fine shoe. It bore the St. Pomfrey foot. The very same foot that—according to these very same newspaper reporters—had tracked down murderers, thieves, and shysters from one side of Europe to another.

The rest of St. Pomfrey was equally impressive—seven feet tall and four hundred pounds heavy. Three tailors spent a week and two bolts of fabric to make each of his silk suits. The ruffles required another bolt.

Incredibly, his massive coiffure, which looked like one of M'Lady Luggertuck's cast-off wigs, was actually his own hair.

The big man moved fast. Walking directly into Hillhemp, Gateberry, and Howbag—knocking one of them down and hurting another's feelings—he strode toward M'Lady Luggertuck.

"Oh, Mr. St. Pomfrey, thank you so much for coming, we—"

"Wait, M'Lady, I beg! Wait for your gilded door to swing closed on its golden hinges and shut out this pack of nosy narwhales! Say not a word!"

And that's just what happened. M'Lady Luggertuck, the valet, several footmen, and Crotty ducked back inside as St. Pomfrey rushed the door, the reporters just behind him.

"Just one quote, please, sir . . ."

"If it's no trouble, sir . . ."

"Is it true that a kitchen boy was . . ."

SLAM!

And that was that. They were outside, and the story, dear Reader, was inside.

12

In Which Horton Scrubs and the Great Detective Detects . . .

And what of Horton Halfpott?

Alas, he was where he was every day at that time. In fact, at almost all times. He was washing dishes.

Imagine how many plates, how many saucers, how many bowls, brandy snifters, butter trays, ice-cube nimbles, gin jiggers, melon ballers, salad tongs, salt cellars, teacups, teakettles, teapots, teaspoons, and tea strainers were used every day at the fancy Luggertuck table, where five-course meals were eaten three times a day, tea was served twice, and midnight snacks were offered at eleven, twelve, and one o'clock.

(You'll notice that forks were not mentioned. Faithful readers will remember that M'Lady Luggertuck had had a fear of forks ever since the events recounted in "M'Lady Luggertuck Hires a Tattooed Nanny.")

The cutlery of the staff has not been mentioned either, but, yes, Horton had to clean their gruel spoons, too. He counted once and found that he washed 652 spoons in a single day.

Yet try as she might—and she might—Miss Neversly never found a spot on any dish Horton cleaned. He was too careful. Miss Neversly once thought she beheld a spot on a sardine tray and beat Horton with her spoon. Then she realized it was only her own shriveled, hateful face reflected in the squeaky-clean surface. This made her so mad she hit him again.

So picture Horton, standing on a bucket, scrubbing away and dreaming of a beautiful girl on a bicycle. Yes, Reader, even if we're not dwelling on the subject, Horton certainly was. The boy was smitten.

"I wish I could see her again," he thought. "I wouldn't even have to talk to her. Just see her. I'll bet she'll be beautiful at the ball. But I'll be right here on my bucket while she and Luther dance. No, I won't even get to be in the same room. Unless . . ."

Whack! went a spoon on the back of his head.

"Halfpott! Pay attention!" bellowed Miss Neversly. "Everyone! To the Front Hall! Now!"

Horton did not dare to ask why. Would you? But it certainly seemed an unusual request. He had never set foot in the Front Hall and had assumed he never would.

He wrung out his rag and hung it on a tiny hook that kitchen boys had been hanging their rags on for two centuries.

The rest of the kitchen staff was excited, but Horton did not welcome the interruption, because it only meant that he would have to work later into the night to finish the washing.

In the Front Hall, he and the rest of the staff assembled in a long line. The head cooks and undercooks, the maids, the cleaners, the gardeners, the footmen, the butlers, the valets, the gamekeeper, the boatman, the boatwoman, the ferret comber, the fire stoker, the wig stroker and, of course, the many boys of kitchen, garden, and stable varieties.

Bump squeezed in next to Horton.

"A great big fat detective is here," whispered Bump excitedly. "He asked to see us. He thinks one of us has the Lump."

A chortle broke out behind them, close enough for hot sardine-scented breath to tickle their ears. They froze, prepared for a beating or worse.

"Well said, small stable boy, well said. I am, in point of fact, all three of those things," St. Pomfrey boomed. The boys cringed.

"I am great—perhaps the greatest practitioner of deduction, detection, and misdirection ever to deduce, detect, and misdirect. I am big, though I am the shortest of three brothers. And alas I am fat, thanks to a love of sardines, deviled eggs, and other delicacies.

"Your remark proves your innocence, boy. The guilty party will try to flatter me with lies. You, common stable boy, are a truth-teller. You may go. Hopefully to bathe."

Bump ran off. Horton wished he could go, too.

Portnoy St. Pomfrey chortled again, watching Bump run with a wistful look in his eye. Then he turned and glared at the servants. "The rest of you may *not* go!

One of you has betrayed Smugwick Manor, betrayed M'Lady Luggertuck, betrayed all that is good amongst men. I will root you out like a mongoose in a snake's den. I will peer into your soul and see the Lump within."

His gaze came to rest on Horton. It seemed to linger.

Horton trembled. St. Pomfrey seemed to be peering into his soul at the Lump within!

Of course, Horton hadn't stolen the Lump, but he did have a secret.

A Big Secret!

And it felt like St. Pomfrey knew all about it.

13

In Which Horton Recalls His Secret . . .

Horton's secret actually goes back further than the beginning of this book.

It goes back to a day, several years earlier, when he got lost on his way to the servants' attic after a long night's washing.

It was dark. He was exhausted. He went up one floor too few. He felt for the rusty doorknob of the attic door and his hand touched a glass doorknob instead.

He should not have opened that door. He should

have gone up to the attic where he belonged, where the other boys were already asleep.

But open it he did—just a crack—and peeked in.

An enormous window let in enough moonlight for him to see what he had found. Among the jumble of Peculiar and Unusual Artifacts were a suit of armor, a massive trunk, a partly built model ship, a strange machine with levers and gears, a white raven (stuffed), a painting of a man with a monkey, and the gilded bindings of hundreds and hundreds of books.

Horton closed the door immediately, found his way back to the stairs, and went up to bed.

But he did not sleep. He kept thinking about all those books and Peculiar and Unusual Artifacts. What else might be in the room, he wondered. He wanted a closer look at the painting and maybe a chance to fiddle with the strange machine and rummage in the big trunk.

Horton's faithfulness and obedience have been spoken of before. And yes, they were strong enough to resist the temptations of a Sweet Sugarapple Pie.

But they were not quite strong enough to keep Horton from the call of those books. He went back to the room the next night.

It was late. Everyone else had gone to bed. He took several candle stubs from the pile of discarded candles. M'Lady Luggertuck insisted on using brand-new candles every night, so there were always plenty of half-used candles around. The better servants used these until they dwindled to tiny stubs. Only then were the lowest servants, such as Horton and Bump, allowed to use the stubs to light their way up to the attic.

Horton lit one of those runty candles at the kitchen fire and climbed the narrow, winding stairs. He found the mysterious room again, peeked through the keyhole to be sure it was unoccupied, turned the glass doorknob, and went inside.

First he looked at the stuffed raven. A little plaque read mervyn, beloved pet.

Then he opened the trunk, full of souvenirs from a trip to some foreign land. There were rolls of paper with strange letters on them, a smoking pipe as long as Horton's left arm, a scary mask, and a long silk robe embroidered with dragons and mermaids.

By the light of his candle he squinted at old books about Norse mythology, amazing science experiments of ancient Persia, Egyptian tomb-building, pirates,

India, King Arthur, and the history of turnips. (The history of turnips is much more interesting than you'd guess.)

By the way, Reader, you may have assumed that Horton could not read. But his father had once been a scholar and had taught Horton how to read and write. That was before his father got sick and his books had been sold to buy medicines that hadn't worked.

Thus, Horton was immersed in a book about pirates when the glass doorknob turned and the door to the room opened.

Ah, Reader, don't let me startle you with my little tricks.

There's nothing to fear here. The door was opened by kindly Old Lord Emberly Luggertuck.

"What ho? Who's this?" he cried. "Not another ghost, I hope."

"I'm a kitchen boy."

"The ghost of a kitchen boy or a live kitchen boy?" asked the old man, who looked much like your grandfather only with a walrus mustache. He lit an enormous oil lamp in the shape of a monkey taking a bath.

“A live kitchen boy, Lord Emberly, sir,” said Horton. “I’m so sorry, sir.”

“Sorry for what?”

“I’ve been reading your books, sir,” he said. “Please, sir, if you’ll let me keep my job, I’ll promise never to come back here again.”

“My boy, you are most welcome to come here as often as you like and read all the books you like. I only wish my grandson, Luther, would do the same. I doubt the boy has ever read a book.”

Lord Emberly settled into a leather chair and propped up his feet on the shell of an enormous tortoise. (The tortoise, alas, was long deceased from natural causes. Someday remind me to tell you the story of how this very same tortoise, nicknamed Daphne, prevented Attila the Hun from capturing the fortress of Rei Ruam.)

“Yes, young Halfpott,” continued Lord Emberly. “I hope you do come back and read all the books you want. But you must never tell anyone about this room. No one knows I sneak back here some nights. If M’Lady hears about it, she’ll throw a fit.”

And so young Horton and Old Lord Emberly Luggertuck shared the library from then on. Sometimes

Horton would read while Lord Emberly tinkered with the strange machine, which turned out to be a giant cuckoo clock. Sometimes Horton would tinker while Lord Emberly told him tales of his many travels and adventures.

And Horton always kept his promise not to reveal Lord Emberly's secret, though he would have loved to have told Bump all about it.

He knew that if M'Lady ever found out, he and Lord Emberly would both regret it.

14

In Which St. Pomfrey's Bluff Is Called . . .

Horton blinked.

He was still in the Front Hall and Portnoy St. Pomfrey was still staring at him.

But now Horton saw that St. Pomfrey's eagle eye was actually rather sleepy-looking. He realized that St. Pomfrey didn't know his secret. Or much else, for that matter.

He was right. St. Pomfrey had not seen into Horton's soul. In fact, he had not seen into anyone's soul. The great detective was bluffing.

St. Pomfrey merely hoped to scare the guilty party

into returning the Lump. That night, the detective planned to hide in the Lump Room and wait for the culprit, probably a footman or a kitchen boy, to tiptoe in.

Tomorrow morning the case would be solved. He would receive a large reward and then invite the reporters in to hear an embellished version of the story that would end with him grappling with a knife-wielding thief.

Many of his cases, including the famous Mystery of the Gold-Plated Umbrella Stand had been solved in this manner.

Ah, but this case won't be solved so easily.

St. Pomfrey did spend the night hiding in the Lump Room. But no one tiptoed in to return the Lump. And even if they had, St. Pomfrey wouldn't have seen them, for the World's Greatest Detective had fallen asleep behind a credenza.

Not only had the Lump not been returned, but Old Crotty soon discovered that someone had ransacked M'Lady Luggertuck's writing desk!

This upset M'Lady Luggertuck greatly, since she had several letters in that desk that it would have been best if no one else had ever read. (See "M'Lady Luggertuck Meets a Handsome Frenchman.")

15

In Which Bump Is Called to Serve . . .

The next day, Colonel Sitwell awoke to find that his monocle had been stolen.

Some of the footmen suggested that the colonel had merely misplaced it, but, since I know how the story is supposed to end, I'm reasonably certain that it was indeed stolen.

The poor colonel could barely see, yet somehow he managed to soldier on—eating and napping with his usual gusto.

Crotty's keys—which opened every door, gate, and

secret passage in the castle—disappeared the day after that.

And the following morning a valuable bust of Napoleon was reported missing from the Front Hall.

Portnoy St. Pomfrey felt a prickle of alarm. Not so much of a prickle that he would actually begin to exert any energy himself. No, 'twas not that prickly. However, he did begin to realize that someone must start investigating.

He sent for Bump.

"Mr. Bump, you have about you the fragrance of *equus poopus,* or in the common tongue, horse manure," he said when Bump arrived.

"Yes, sir," replied Bump. "I spend most of my days shoveling it."

"I see," replied the Great Detective, peering down at the small, sandy-haired lad. "Aside from that aforementioned odor, you remind me of myself when I was your age. Keen-eyed and clever, with a streak of curiosity that would either make me famously rich or famously dead."

"Really?" asked Bump, wide-eyed with excitement.

"Yes, son, yes," said Portnoy St. Pomfrey, who used this same speech whenever he needed cheap help.

“I imagine you’ve heard that I will receive a large reward for my invaluable services when I find the Lump.”

“Yes, sir.”

“Would you like some of that money?”

“Me, sir?”

“Yes, my boy, I need someone swift of foot, eye, and ear to find the clues, the tiny details, the overheard comments that will allow my celebrated cerebellum to solve this terrible crime,” said St. Pomfrey. (What he really wanted was someone to eavesdrop on the other servants.) “Can you do that? And can you find one or two of your little friends to help, too? You’ll all get a share of the reward if you bring me Valuable Clues.”

“Yes, sir, of course, sir!”

St. Pomfrey’s plan of hiring Bump was a good one—better, in fact, than he could have guessed—but it did not bring immediate results. Another ghastly crime was at that very moment being discovered.

Hark, is that the sound of a bellowing M’Lady Luggertuck that I hear? Yes, it is. Corset or not, she was in a Raging Fury and was looking for someone to sink her (false) teeth into.

16

In Which the Purple Sanctity of the Wig Room Is Violated . . .

I have chosen, Reader, not to burden you with descriptions of the rooms of Smugwick Manor, other than Lord Emberly's. They were, mostly, filled with boring old junk like end tables and flower vases and bric-a-brac. Some were recently remodeled by M'Lady Luggertuck and revealed the most appalling taste. (See "M'Lady Luggertuck Brings Fashion to Smugwick Manor.") The lamps were particularly hideous.

One room, however, merits description, yet almost defies it—the Wig Room.

In decorating her Wig Room, M'Lady Luggertuck had decided that plaster, paint, rugs, and wallpaper were too common. Thus the entire room—floor, walls, and ceiling—was upholstered in purple velvet. The purple was deeper than any purple you or I have ever seen. In fact, you or I might call it black, but the clever London shopkeeper who sold it to M'Lady Luggertuck insisted that it was indeed a deep, deep, deep purple.

The room held just a single chair, but, Reader, what a chair! 'Struth, it was a throne for M'Lady to rest in while Old Crotty and the Wig Keepers fitted M'Lady's wigs to M'Lady's head.

Each chair leg was a dancing goat carved from ivory, then gilded with pure gold. The arms were swans' necks and the seat back bore a tapestry of Jason holding the Golden Fleece.

The seat cushion was so soft that M'Lady Luggertuck would sink down and sometimes get stuck.

Surrounding the chair were pedestals, also covered

in purple velvet. Each held a gleaming, polished porcelain Wig Head.

Atop each Wig Head was, of course, one of M'Lady Luggertuck's wigs.

Every shade and style of hair currently fashionable was represented. This one was named the "The Parisian Wing." That one was "The Follicle Fantasy." And over there, looming high above the rest, was the famed wig known as "Colossus o' Curls." And so on. (Wigs that fell out of fashion were buried in a sacred spot on the Smugwick estate.)

Each week the Assistant Wig Keeper hauled up two twenty-five-pound sacks of wig chalk just to keep them all properly powdered.

Imagine the Assistant Wig Keeper's surprise as she staggered into the room with her heavy sacks and saw that one of the Wig Heads was bald!

Yes, bald! Sometime during the night, a thief had slipped into the Wig Room and defiled that heavenly hair haven by stealing the Colossus o' Curls.

17

In Which Trouble Furrows the Luggertuck Brow . . .

I feel certain that the theft in the Wig Room explains the aforementioned Raging Fury of M'Lady Luggertuck, who had decided to sink her (false) teeth into Portnoy St. Pomfrey.

St. Pomfrey was trying to sink his teeth into an anchovy-stuffed deviled egg. I fear he did not enjoy it as much as he hoped.

M'Lady Luggertuck, wearing a second-best wig, roared at him across the dinner table. "Mr. Pumfley, a

Fashionable Wig has been stolen from right under your nose!"

St. Pomfrey's hand shook and an eggy bit fell off his spoon and onto his silk suit, ruining in one instant the product of a week's patient labor by the three tailors.

M'Lady roared on. She cared not for the patient labor of the three tailors.

"Shall I inform the reporters stationed on my lawn that you have not only failed to find the Lump, but you have failed to make this household safe for Fashionable Wigs?"

"I would prefer, M'Lady, if confidentiality could prevail until all the facts have been sifted and—"

"By the time you, sir, have sifted all the facts, I shall be Wigless and stripped stark naked by thieves!"

This was an eventuality no one wanted.

M'Lady continued. "How difficult can it be to figure out which servant has possession of a three-foot-tall wig fashioned from twenty-three pounds of real human hair?"

"Ah, M'Lady, it may not be a servant."

The Luggertuck eyes flashed and St. Pomfrey's spoon fell to the floor with an eggy clatter.

"Of course it's a servant," M'Lady spat. "You don't think a member of my own family would steal my wig, do you?"

Luther, who had been unusually quiet during this exchange, began to choke guiltily on a caviar-filled scone.

But St. Pomfrey was too flustered to notice.

"Nay, nay, M'Lady. Certainly your own family is above suspicion. However I have received reports of pirates in these parts. Perhaps one of these brigands—"

M'Lady Luggertuck interrupted venomously.

"Pirates? Really, Mr. St. Pumfley. We're one hundred miles from the ocean."

M'Lady Luggertuck began to wonder if St. Pomfrey really deserved his fame. She began compiling mean-spirited remarks about his detective methods, intelligence, and personal hygiene, which she would spread amongst the other m'ladies of the land if necessary and possibly even if not necessary.

In the meantime, she could only sit around and shout. Which she did for the remainder of breakfast.

Though her shouting took its toll on St. Pomfrey's nerves and digestion, M'Lady felt a little disappointed in the tone and timbre of it. She simply failed to hit the high notes.

She needed her corset tightened, she realized, and was just about to ask Crotty to do so when Footman Jennings announced the presence of visitors.

"Well, who on earth is it?" asked M'Lady irritably.

In his most official voice, Footman Jennings announced, "Duchess Carolyn Crimcramper and her son Master Montgomery Crimcramper."

"Egad," muttered M'Lady as her visitors entered.

Egad, indeed. Had you forgotten? The duchess is the one who started all the fuss by asking if her son, Montgomery, might stay in order to be closer to Miss Celia Sylvan-Smythe.

Though the ball was yet a week away, Montgomery's mother hoped he could get in several visits with Miss Sylvan-Smythe to lay the groundwork for a proposal the night of the ball.

Reader, I must warn you. Montgomery is such a dull character that, if he did not play such an important part in the story, I would have left him out. His mother is dull, too. In fact, you're welcome to forget her. There are enough characters for you to remember as it is.

You'll recall that Luther Luggertuck appeared to hate Montgomery—"ugh" was his assessment of his cousin's character—but now he will pretend to like him.

"I'll offer to show him around," Luther said to himself. "I'll offer to be friends, and, oh yes, offer to accompany Montgomery on his visits to Miss Sylvan-Smythe. Next to him, even I will shine like a star. Perhaps she will fall madly in love with me and I won't need the plan after all. Oh, but it's such a delicious plan."

For Montgomery's part, his brain simply worked too rarely to realize that Luther might be competition.

And so Montgomery and Luther became summertime chums. Ignorance and Evil—an ugly alliance.

18

In Which Napoleon Returns . . .

A meeting was held that afternoon in the loft above the stables. A roll call was not taken, but would have gone like this: Bump, here. Blight, here. Blemish, here. Horton, absent. (Horton had too many gherkin tongs to polish.)

"It's certainly too bad Horton could not be here," said Blemish.

"He's got a stack of dishes a mile high!" complained Bump.

“I’m afraid that all the extra guests in the manor are making his job truly Sisyphean,” said Blight.

“What’s that mean?” asked Bump.

“It means he’ll work and work and never get it all done. The guests dirty the dishes faster than he can clean them.”

“They sure do. It’s so unfair! Why do they make him do it all himself?” lamented Bump.

“Such a nice fellow, too,” said Blight. “I wish we could find a way to aid him.”

“Actually,” said Bump more cheerfully, “maybe we can share our reward with him!”

“To what reward do you refer?” asked Blemish.

Bump told Blight and Blemish of his talk with the Great Detective and of the man’s offer to share the reward for finding the Lump.

“If we find it, we’ll be rich!” cried Blemish, so excited he forgot to talk in a butlery way. “We can get Horton out of the kitchen! And get ourselves out of these stinky stables!”

“Ahem,” said Blight, disapproving of Blemish’s use of the slang term “stinky.” “My colleague’s grammar notwithstanding, I do heartily concur that we must secure the Lump and, in turn, a share of the reward."

Blemish still could not control his enthusiasm.

"Let's go!" he cried. "Let's start looking right now!"

"Shh," said Bump. "We need to be quiet about this. Clever, too. The butlers have already searched the castle and the stables and the gardens. I doubt we'll find it by chance."

"Then what do we do?"

"I think we should try to discover who did it, then follow the thief and see if he leads us to it."

"Well, I don't think it was one of us servants," said Blemish, beginning to regain his butlery composure. "None of us, to put it quite bluntly, believes the Lump is really a diamond, except perhaps Old Crotty. And it is my opinion that she would never steal from the Luggertucks. Not in a million years."

"Good point," said Bump, impressed. "Perhaps it was a burglar."

"That leads me to ask," said Blight. "Why would a burglar steal a frumpy wig, a monocle, and a bust of Napoleon? After all, there must be something in the manor worth more than that . . . er . . . stuff."

"Good point," said Bump, again impressed. He'd never before realized how bright Blight and Blemish were. "That means it must have been one of the Luggertucks or Colonel Sitwell."

"Sir and M'Lady would have no reason to steal the Lump," said Blight, "and the colonel is not inclined to put forth the necessary exertions. Plus, why would he purloin his own eyepiece?"

"What?" said Bump, getting a little lost in all the butlery talk, not to mention a little annoyed.

"If I may use the common term for his condition, he means that Colonel Sitwell is too *lazy* to steal, and has no motive," said Blemish.

"I see," said Bump, "well, that leaves Luther."

"I, for one, am not at all surprised," said Blight.

Blemish seconded this. "I'll wager he's too greedy to wait until he lawfully inherits the Lump. But why would he steal the wig and those other things?"

"That's what we'll have to figure out," said Bump. "From now on, one of us will be watching him all the time. The other two will cover that person's chores."

"I'll go first," said both Blight and Blemish at the same time.

They drew straws and Blight won. They decided he should start immediately.

Because stable boys were not allowed in the nicer parts of the house, he needed to be very sneaky. He hid behind a tapestry of the Battle of Hastings, which hung near Luther's room, and watched the door for the rest of the day, but, as Blight discovered by way of the keyhole, all Luther did was sleep until dinner.

After following Luther to the dining room, Blight gave up. He returned to the stables.

"Verily, that was the most boring afternoon I've spent in my whole life," he told the others. "I must own that I would have preferred to have been shoveling horse manure."

"Very good, Mr. Blight. Here you go then," said Blemish, handing him the shovel with a chuckle.

Blemish didn't see anything interesting either until just after midnight. Shortly after various clocks had struck twelve, Luther emerged from his bedroom, carrying a single candle and something big and heavy under his arm.

Blemish, hiding behind a tapestry of the Second

Battle of Hastings, held his breath as Luther walked past, just inches away.

Then, as quietly as he could manage, he crept after Luther.

Suddenly Luther stopped and sniffed. He looked all around for the source of the smell.

Blemish, the source of the smell, slipped into M'Lady Luggertuck's Spare Corset Closet just in time.

Luther continued on and so did Blemish. They went down a winding staircase and along the Creepy Hall of Luggertuck Portraits. Ah, if only Blemish had had a chance to look at the paintings! Surely he would have noticed the resemblance betwixt Bump and Great Uncle Wilkerson Luggertuck, Earl of Swinetusk.

But Luther passed by the paintings and tiptoed down the Grand Staircase to the Front Hall, and thus so did Blemish. He crouched at the foot of the stairs and watched as Luther approached the mantelpiece above the Great Big Fireplace.

Luther grunted as he raised the heavy object he had been carrying up onto the mantelpiece. But it was simply too dark for Blemish to see what it was.

Then Luther turned and headed up the Grand Staircase again. Luckily, in the darkness, he mistook Blemish for the Grand Newel Post.

As soon as Luther left, Blemish ran to find a candle, then rushed back to see what Luther had put on the mantel.

There was no mistaking the beady eyes that peered down at him. Napoleon had returned! Luther had unstolen the bust.

19

In Which Horton Falls in Again . . .

On Sunday, just one week before the ball, Horton rose early and took his customary trip to his family's house.

The two halves of the journey—one to the house and the other back to Smugwick Manor—were very, very different.

The trip home was always filled with a week's worth of hopes. Hope that something good had happened to his family. Hope that his father had gotten better. Hope that the family finally had enough money for a doctor.

Instead, he would find his family always a little worse off than the week before. The little cottage always a little bit more rundown as Uncle Lemuel got too old to fix the things that broke. And his father never any better.

Thus the trip back to Smugwick Manor was always gloomy. It also meant that he had to face another week of Miss Neversly and fetching firewood and washing dishes and on and on.

Sometimes, he envied Bump, Blight, and Blemish. Since they didn't have families, they just slept late on Sunday mornings. They had nothing to look forward to except well-earned rest, but they also had no disappointments.

This week Horton had faced more than the usual disappointments. His father was worse, Uncle Lemuel had hurt his leg while trying to patch the roof, and one of the goats had run off. His mother had found it hard to smile when he gave her the penny and she, as usual, had to tell him that, no, it still wasn't enough.

And so, Horton's spirits were particularly low as he made the return trip to Smugwick Manor.

Then, as he approached Magpie Pond, where he would leave the road to take the shortcut through

Wolfleg Woods, he saw something that made him feel better.

First he saw the bicycle, then the rider. It was Miss Celia Sylvan-Smythe again, throwing rocks into the pond. Not skipping them, mind you, but lofting them high in the air so they made big splashes.

"Mr. Halfpott! Mr. Halfpott!" she called.

"Good afternoon, ma'am," he said. He felt that he should slip on past. He felt that he shouldn't be talking to her.

But he couldn't have gotten by, because she actually ran forward to greet him.

"No, no. Don't you remember? I'm not a ma'am, just a miss. I'd be glad to be called Celia, but I suppose since we just met you should call me Miss Sylvan-Smythe."

"I'd like that, Miss Sylvan-Smythe." Horton grinned in spite of himself. In spite of propriety. In spite of the fact that we're not supposed to be dwelling on this subject.

She grinned back.

"Where have you been, Mr. Halfpott?"

"I've been to see my family."

"Oh, I hope they're well."

Properly, Horton should have said, "Yes, thank you, Miss."

But there was something irresistible in Celia's manner—in her voice and her eyes. Something that told him he would find real sympathy here and, on that day, he needed it.

"No," he murmured, "my father is very sick. He's been sick for a long time."

"What does the doctor say?" she asked.

Horton was ashamed to tell her that his family hadn't been able to pay for a doctor in years.

Celia—being a very clever girl, after all—understood right away. And she formed a plan of action right away, too, but she decided to keep that to herself for the moment.

A hasty change of subjects was needed.

"Thank you for giving me that invitation to the ball. I'm coming as Little Bo-peep. What will you wear?"

Alas, Celia's new subject caused the same problems as the old one.

It set off a chain of conflicting emotions in Horton, putting him over the daily quota of conflicting emotions that a person can be expected to endure gracefully.

Just talking to Miss Sylvan-Smythe mixed embarrassment and happiness, with happiness ahead by a nose. But to imagine that she wanted to see him at the ball was joy and shame wrapped in one. Joy because he would of course love to see her at the ball, too. Shame because he would be scrubbing the guests' dirty dishes down in the kitchen while she danced in the ballroom.

He couldn't speak.

"Oh," she asked, "is your costume a secret?"

"No," he stammered. "I don't have a costume. I—"

He heard horses approaching behind him. If someone saw him talking to Miss Celia Sylvan-Smythe, he'd be in big trouble. He'd better get going.

Then he heard a voice behind him. He'd tarried too long.

"Here now! Boy!"

He'd been caught, he realized, and he had a bad feeling he knew who'd done the catching.

"You're one of our kitchen boys, aren't you?"

Horton turned around. Yes, just as he had feared,

it was Luther Luggertuck. And Montgomery was with him.

Worse than the knowledge of the trouble he was in was the fact that Miss Sylvan-Smythe would soon understand just how lowly his status was. Humiliation loomed!

"We don't pay you to loiter around the pond with your friends," snarled Luther.

What a statement! They hardly paid him at all, and it was his day off!

Luther and Montgomery dismounted. Luther, who had not yet met Miss Celia Sylvan-Smythe, was being elbowed in the ribs by Montgomery, who had.

"Luther, that's her! That's Sylvan-Smythe," Montgomery whispered, too loudly.

Luther was stunned. Why was the richest young lady in fifty miles talking to a kitchen boy? He was too unfamiliar with the concepts of friendship and love to suspect the truth, but he certainly suspected something.

He had merely planned to tease the kitchen boy, but now he realized that the servant must be put in his proper place. The handiest proper place, it occurred to Luther, was the muddy waters of Magpie Pond.

But Luther's cleverness ran too deep to let his emotions make him look brutish in front of a young lady. That was what Montgomery was for.

"Montgomery, that kitchen boy is pestering your future bride. Best go to her rescue," he whispered to Montgomery, not too loudly. "I recommend you toss him in yonder pond."

"That doesn't sound very nice," said Montgomery.

"The young lady's honor is at stake," hissed Luther, whose own claim to honor ran thinner than the servants' gruel.

"Oh," said Montgomery. "Well, I guess I'd better do something then." He clomped forward.

Horton figured he had just enough time to run, but he didn't move.

Instead, acting on an impulse, he turned back around and looked directly at Miss Celia Sylvan-Smythe. He said quietly, "I think you'll look very beautiful as Little Bo-peep. I hope you have a wonderful time."

Then an even more outlandish impulse prompted him to whisper, "Maybe I'll see you there," just as a big, meaty hand grabbed him by the neck, pulled him backward, and flung him into the pond.

20

In Which the Alliance Faces an Early Setback . . .

Horton clambered out of the pond, muddy again. Humiliated? Yes, but not as humiliated as if he had just run away. But he also knew that lingering couldn't possibly help.

"Good day, Master Luther, Master Montgomery, Miss Sylvan-Smythe," he said, looking at the ground, and began walking briskly along the path to Smugwick Manor.

Since he owned no other set of clothes, the rest

of the day would be spent feeling damp and clammy. Ah, but how warm he would have felt if he could have heard the conversation that took place after he left.

"Miss Sylvan-Smythe, what a pleasure to see you again," Montgomery said. "I'm so sorry that you've been disturbed by one of Luggertuck's servants."

"I, too, am sorry," she replied, looking not at Montgomery but at Horton disappearing into the woods. "However, my regret is double. First, that he was disturbed by you and, second, that now I am as well. You address me by name. Have we been introduced?"

Montgomery, struggling to keep up with her words, missed their meaning.

"Yes, yes, we danced a waltz at Madame Madelyn's Spring Gala in London. Don't you remember?"

"Thankfully, no."

Luther cleared his throat and edged forward, standing as straight as he could despite years of bad posture from slithering around Smugwick Manor.

"Oh, yes," said Montgomery, "this is my cousin, Luther Luggertuck. Luther, this is Miss Sylvan-Smythe."

"What a pleasure," Luther said. "I find that your

beauty, which I have heard so much about, has been greatly understated." And he reached forward as if to take her hand and draw it to his lips.

Well, Reader? You know a little of Miss Sylvan-Smythe by now. Do you think she is likely to listen to this transparent flattery?

Of course not. She jerked her hand away.

Luther tried again.

"I do hope you'll be attending my mother's costume ball."

"Yes," she replied, "there is someone I very much wish to see there."

"What will your costume be?" asked Luther. "Perhaps Lady Godiva?"

"Certainly not!" replied Celia, outraged and very tempted to slap Luther, except she'd never slapped anyone before. "I'll be dressed as Little Bo-peep. Please excuse me; I must be going."

Luther tried again.

"As a matter of fact, Montgomery and I had thought to pay a call on the Shortleys, in hopes of finding you there. May we accompany you?"

“Do not bother,” she said. “Do not bother accompanying me, and do not bother visiting the Shortleys.”

And she got on her bicycle and sped off.

“I think she likes me,” said Montgomery.

Luther was glad he had a plan.

21

In Which Lord Emberly Luggertuck Delivers a Story and a Warning . . .

Horton sought to put the day's humiliations behind him by turning to a good book.

He washed the dishes as quickly as he could but was still the last to leave the kitchen.

He lit one of his candle stumps to light the way to Lord Emberly's study, but when he arrived he found it already aglow. Lord Emberly was there talking to Mervyn, the deceased white raven.

"I saw the herons again today, Mervyn," he

whispered. "Also two hawks, several finches, and that lark you used to like so much. Ah, I wish I could see you two flying together again."

"Good evening, Lord Emberly," called Horton.

"Ah, young Mr. Halfpott," replied the old man. "I hoped to see you tonight. Something is troubling me."

Poor Horton. His first thought was always to blame himself. He assumed Lord Emberly must be displeased with him for one or another of his recent misadventures, perhaps even suspected him of stealing the Lump.

"I heard from Mr. West, the gamekeeper, that you had a run-in with my grandson, Luther. Apparently it's the talk of the manor."

Now Horton felt sick. Lord Emberly had heard about his impolite behavior—talking to a young lady, disobeying a young gentleman. Now, he knew, the ax would fall. He would be barred from the study, perhaps dismissed from his job.

He stammered out an apology.

"No, Horton, I'm the one who's sorry," rumbled Lord Emberly. "Sorry that the evil young weasel bears my name, the once-great Luggertuck name. You have my apology, if not his."

This unexpected sympathy made Horton begin to cry.

This was a little embarrassing to Lord Emberly who, though kindly, had little experience with unfortunate young persons. His own son was a vacant twit and his grandson, as has been noted, was an evil weasel. Neither one ever merited much sympathy.

Lord Emberly patted Horton on the shoulder, then began to tell a story.

"You know, it was Luther who drove me out of the manor.

"His mother, the so-called M'Lady Luggertuck is truly a terrible woman, but when she gave birth to Luther I dreamed that he might be a proper grandson. But everything I tried to do for the boy ended with him running to his mother, bawling. The kite string hurt his hand. The rocking horse rocked too much. The top didn't spin right.

"Once, I tried to build him a tree house in the Big Ugly Oak Tree down by the mire. It started well enough. I carried the lumber and the tools, but I thought I'd try to make a man of him, so I asked him to help. I gave him a single board to carry. A single board, mind you.

"He began whining about what hard work it was before we were out of the garden. By the time we reached the mire he was calling me names. Then, just as I reached the edge of the mire, I received a mighty wallop on my backside. The little demon had whacked me with his board! I lost my balance and fell in.

"I looked up to see him toss the board into a bush, stick out his tongue, and run back down the path crying for his mother.

"By the time I climbed out of the stinking mud and returned to the manor, he had concocted a scandalous story, casting me as a villainous brute who had tried to lose him in the mire. Frankly, I wish I had.

"That was the last straw for me. I gave up on the lot of them, including my own son, Whimperton. I'll never know why he married that woman and I'll never know how he sired such a devilish child.

"That's when I moved into the assistant gamekeeper's cottage, where I've been much happier."

Horton felt much better knowing that he wasn't the only one who'd been foully treated by Luther, nor the only one to have fallen in the mire.

"But, Horton," continued Lord Emberly, "I'm afraid

it might not be so easy for you. If Luther has decided he doesn't like you, he might do something very nasty. He's capable of anything. He's had many servants fired and several jailed, and one or two mysteriously vanished. You must be extremely careful."

Lord Emberly, great man that he was—a hero of various expeditions to unscaled mountains, unnavigable rivers, and uncharted jungles—gave a brief shudder and added one last chilling warning:

"And if you upset his mother, you really will be in trouble."

22

In Which Three Young Sleuths Trail a Sloth . . .

After the initial excitement of seeing Luther with the bust of Napoleon, Bump, Blight, and Blemish discovered that trailing the idle brat was boring to the point of agony.

To think that during all those long days while they worked in the stables, this cretin did nothing but sleep, slouch, slink, and slime his way around the manor and whine to his mother for his allowance!

While they went hungry between an early breakfast

of gruel and a late supper of bread crust, singular, he filled the time between his lavish meals gulping Candied Quail Eggs by the handful!

Worst of all, they witnessed him abusing the servants. He leered at Milly the new maid, he whacked his valet on the head with a cane, and he even tripped poor Old Crotty. Any of these people, even Crotty, could have beaten Luther in a fair fight. But because they were servants and he was a gentleman, they could not defend themselves.

The stable boys had not found any evidence to connect Luther to the crime of stealing the Lump, but all agreed that his whole life amounted to one long, lazy crime against decency, his fellow man, nature, the British Isles, the Queen, and even the Luggertuck name, which wasn't so great to start with.

Somehow, Bump thought, they were better off when they had not known just how good Luther had it and how little he deserved to have it so.

Bump usually took daytime Luther duty because, even without the cloak of dark night draped o'er the manor, he was very, very good at trailing Luther unnoticed. The tiny boy would flicker like a shadow from behind a vase, scoot under a table, or slip through a door left ajar, never losing sight of his quarry. And he was a mighty clever fellow. As he waited for Luther, his mind was busy fitting together the pieces of this mystery.

On this particular hot and sticky afternoon, as Bump stood behind the musty tapestry outside Luther's door, he began to think the lazybones would never stir from his bedchamber. But he was wrong. The door opened, the weasel emerged, and the chase began: Down the third back staircase, through the Hall of Taxidermy, past the statue of Sir Falstaff Luggertuck (which was turned toward the wall because the nose had fallen off), and then through a door that Bump had never seen before.

Yet, once through it, Bump realized he was standing in the Vestibule of Large Roman Things. He had heard tell of it from Horton and some of the other servants. Several generations earlier, a Luggertuck lord had been obsessed with collecting examples of ancient Roman masonry—bricks, broken columns, the occasional besandaled foot and leg of a Caryatid statue. Now nobody knew what to do with all of it, so the Large

Roman Things sat in this unused room and, for all I know, they may be sitting there to this day.

As Bump slipped into the room and slid behind a column, he watched Luther approach a mosaic that covered an entire wall. The mosaic, made out of thousands of small tiles, formed a picture of Hercules completing one of his twelve tasks—The Cleansing of the Augean Stables. Bump thought this was the greatest piece of art he'd ever seen.

Luther moved forward and removed a largish tile from just under Hercules's bulging arm muscle. (Yes, it was his mighty Armpit, but I didn't want to come right out and say that.) Then he—Luther, not Hercules—selected a key from the large key ring he had stolen from Old Crotty and inserted it into the hole. He turned the key and the entire wall swung open like a big door.

Luther walked through, leaving the door open behind him. Silently, Bump followed.

As they walked down a long, twisting passageway, the light grew dimmer and dimmer until nothing could be seen at all. Suddenly, Bump realized that Luther's scuffling footsteps had stopped.

Bump had been following too closely. He was only a few feet from Luther, who was rustling around in the dark. Bump didn't move or breathe or blink.

He heard the sound of papers being pushed aside and then a strange soft sound and a clink.

Then Bump heard Luther's footsteps again, but this time Luther was walking toward him. The tiny stable boy sank to the ground and pushed himself up against the wall. As Luther walked past, Bump felt something hairy drag across his arm, but Luther kept walking.

"By M'Lady's Bunions! He almost got me," thought Bump. "I've pushed my luck too far. I've got to be more careful or I'll wind up throttled by that villain."

Being careful, Reader, is usually good. But in times of evil deeds, sometimes a stable boy must be bold. Bump had been bold so far and had come out all right. Now he had lost his nerve, and that's a bad thing to lose when you're in a tight, dark secret passage with an evil Luggertuck.

This time Bump didn't follow Luther so closely, and he felt for each step to be sure he didn't trip in the dark.

Gradually it got a little lighter as they neared the

open door. Bump realized he had fallen far behind Luther.

But not so far behind that he couldn't now see what Luther held in his hand—an elaborate, ridiculous, ugly-as-a-wet-gopher wig.

"He *is* the wig thief! He must have hidden it in here for safekeeping," Bump thought.

That was a very good thought and a correct one, but alas, this was not a time for thinking. It was a time for action, because Luther was pushing the heavy door shut.

Bump wasn't close enough to slip out. The door shut with a heavy thunk and the lock slipped back into place with a rusty clank.

Bump was trapped.

23

In Which a Simple Errand Turns Smelly and Scary . . .

M'Lady Luggertuck suddenly decided that she wanted to add leg of lamb to the smorgasbord being prepared for the ball. (She'd had a hankering for lamb lately. The loosening of her corset had done wonders for her appetite.)

Miss Neversly, who had already purchased a wagonload of food for the party, had not bought any lamb legs, so she dispatched Horton to the village to buy one from the butcher.

Old Crotty reluctantly gave him a coin to pay for the lamb leg. The coin was of such a high value that Horton did not even recognize it. It would have been very easy for him to simply take the coin and leave forever. To his family such a coin would seem like a fortune and the Luggertucks would never miss it. (Although M'Lady would eventually miss her lamb leg.)

But we know Horton too well to entertain such a notion, however appealing it may be.

He got the lamb leg all right, but something strange happened as he returned from the village with the nicely wrapped meat. Something never before seen anywhere in those parts.

Pirates were afoot, and Horton was the first to see them.

Pirates? you ask. In a landlocked county in the near-middle of England?

Horton asked himself the same question as chills ran up his spine and fear waded through his stomach.

Of course he'd never seen pirates before, but he'd read about them in Lord Emberly's books, and the motley group clomping down the road looked just right—long knives, leathery skin, broken noses, filthy clothes, earrings, lice, scabs, nose hair. An unmistakable odor of old fish wafted toward him in the air.

"Hey, boy, you got some meat there?" one called as they drew near.

Horton nodded.

"Hand it over, then," growled the brigand, a burly, bearded fellow carrying, of all things, an anchor.

"Oh, no, please, sir," said Horton, desperate. "It's not mine. I've got to take it up to the castle. Please, sir, I'll get a real beating if I don't bring it back with me."

"Hmmm, what do you say, Cap'n Splinterlock?" said the bearded man to a tall, handsome gentleman with an enormous scar on his back. Horton couldn't see the scar, of course, but it was there all right.

"Don't worry, lad," cried the captain in a booming voice more appropriate for use on board a ship during a typhoon or a mutiny. "Servants we all were once upon a time when our teeth were still in our skulls and not littering the seafloor along with Roland's leg and Harvey's thumbs."

Horton noticed a peg-legged man and a thumbless man wincing at this comment.

The captain continued:

"Steal that meat off your master's table, aye, we might do that, but we'll not steal it from you."

"Thank you, sir," said Horton.

Some of the pirates grumbled.

"Cap'n Splinterlock always takes the fun out of being a pirate," whispered one.

"We're supposed to take whatever we want! Well, I want a leg-o-lamb tonight!"

"Aye, that would taste a lot better than Cap'n's sermons about the Pirate's Code of Honor."

"Quiet back there!" snarled Splinterlock.

"Excuse me," Horton asked, against his better judgment—and mine, too, I should say. "Are you pirates?"

"Aye."

"Where's your boat?"

"Ahhhh," said the captain, finally lowering his voice. "A sore subject you've hit upon. You won't mention it again unless you fancy walking the plank."

Horton assumed this was a joke, as none of the pirates were carrying a plank. However, instead of laughing, several pirates seemed to be fighting back tears. He thought he heard the bearded one with the anchor give a little sigh-like sob.

It was indeed a sore subject, because these were Shipless Pirates. Oh yes, they'd had a ship once. The *Very Scary Shark* had been a fine ship. And the captain was in truth a fine captain. Though he plundered and looted, murdered and maimed, he always did it with a sense of fair play.

Then one night—a dark and stormy one, with rough seas and hurricane winds—they came up behind the infamous pirate ship *Seasickness*.

"Let me hoist the mainsail, come around three points hard a'starboard and give 'em a broadside o' cannon shot," the first mate yelled to the captain through the gale.

"No," Captain Splinterlock hollered back, "that wouldn't be honorable. We'll hold our fire until the storm clears and I'm sure the captain of the *Seasickness* will do the same."

Just then the *Seasickness* opened fire. The *Very Scary Shark* was sunk, and the pirates had to cling to their cargo—stolen barrels of Peruvian Bat Guano—to survive.

Though they would follow their captain to the ends of the Earth, the crew couldn't help resenting his honorable ways, and grumbling about them, as they were now.

"No, no, lads! To the future we sail, not the past," the captain went on, booming again. "A new ship will be ours. We've a little errand to run and a rich reward to claim, then we'll sail again. Right, boys?"

The pirates murmured halfheartedly and began trudging on toward the village.

And that was that, piratically speaking—until Chapter 36.

24

In Which the Alarm Is Raised . . .

Horton decided to stop at the stables before returning to the kitchen with the lamb leg. He wanted to tell Bump and the other boys about the pirates.

He found Blight and Blemish in such a state of panic that they had abandoned butleresque speaking in favor of babbling.

"Bump hasn't come back! He got up early this morning to follow Luther," Blemish said. "Nobody has seen him since. He's hours late."

They told Horton about how they'd been taking turns trailing Luther.

"I've just been to spy on Luther myself," Blight told him. "I peeped through the dining room window and there he was, dribbling wine down the front of his shirt. I didn't see Bump anywhere!"

"Bump should have come to the stables when Luther went in to supper," said Blemish. "In fact, he should have come during Luther's luncheon, too, but he didn't. I'm afraid Luther might have caught him and . . ."

As Blight and Blemish rattled on, Lord Emberly's warning echoed in Horton's ear. Luther was more than just spoiled and rude; he was dangerous. Bump—Horton's best friend in all the world—could be in real trouble.

"We need to find him fast," Horton told the boys.

"But where do we look?" moaned Blight.

"We must look everywhere," said Horton. "We've got to get all the other boys to help us. While Luther and the other Luggertucks are eating, we should be safe to search the house. We'll check every room we can, even the Very Off-Limits ones. The footmen and butlers are very fond of Bump; hopefully they'll let us through."

Blight and Blemish couldn't believe what they were hearing. Horton Halfpott—who wouldn't break the tiniest rule, who wouldn't even eat a slice of Loafburton's Sweet Sugarapple Pie—was planning to lead a mob of filthy stable hands and gardeners through the manor, breaking rules right and left.

In truth, Horton was shocked by his own suggestion. To him the plan seemed almost like mutiny. To the other stable and garden boys—when they were asked to join—it sounded like a good deal of fun. There was no shortage of volunteers.

"We'll start as soon as I've delivered this leg of lamb to the kitchen," declared Horton, before hurrying off toward a sure spoon-beating for lateness from Miss Neversly.

25

In Which Bump Finds Forks, but Not Freedom . . .

Bump worried about getting out, of course. But believe it or not, he had something else on his mind to take care of first.

"If this is where Luther hid the wig," he figured, "maybe this is where he hid the Lump."

He felt his way back down the narrow hallway to the place where he had heard Luther rustling around with some papers.

He found the papers. They felt like envelopes and

a few sheets of writing paper. They smelled like wilted flowers.

I believe I have mentioned Bump's clever brain before. Thus it should be no surprise that he quickly deduced that these were the items stolen from M'Lady Luggertuck's writing desk. He pocketed these as Valuable Clues.

He felt around again, but found nothing more. Luther must be hiding the Lump somewhere else. But where?

Bump sat down to think it out. Then he remembered that he was trapped deep in the innards of Smugwick Manor with no windows, no candles, no food, and possibly very little air. He immediately turned his attention to that problem instead.

He quickly determined that there were no trapdoors hidden in the floor, no iron rungs leading up the wall to an ivy-covered turret, and no iron grate covering an unused ventilation shaft that led to freedom. There was no way out but the way he had come in.

His hopes were raised when he found a small alcove. However, after some fumbling around in the dark, he realized it was lined with shelves and the shelves seemed to be full of silverware. No, not just any silverware, he realized, as he felt around blindly. Forks. No spoons or knives. Just hundreds and hundreds of forks.

Strange, but it was to no immediate purpose.

Bump returned to the wall that Luther had opened. Did he see a small bit of light? Yes!

Luther, being lazy, had forgotten to put the tile back over the keyhole in Hercules's Armpit. Bump could see most of the Vestibule of Large Roman Objects.

It was empty, of course. But since he had nothing better to do, Bump stood and looked through the keyhole, mulling over various Lump-related mysteries all the while.

I hope, Reader, that it will not lessen your appreciation of young Bump's heroic doings if I record here that after two hours he began to cry a little. He was just a young fellow, and he began to think about all the tons and tons of stones and bricks on all sides of him.

After three hours, he imagined that one day Luther would come back through the door and find his tiny skeleton a'lying there and would kick it out of the way.

But he wiped away the tears and kept his eye pressed to the keyhole and kept thinking about what needed to be done when he got out.

After four hours, someone did come into the room. It was a stable boy, Tarpitch, who had joined the search party mostly because he liked the idea of snooping around.

"Tarpitch!" cried Bump.

"What ho, Bump? Where are you? We're all looking for you."

"I'm in Hercules's Armpit."

"What—"

"There's no time to explain. Get Blemish and Blight as fast as you can! Tell them Luther is up to something. They must follow him wherever he goes tonight. Oh, and also, tell Horton where I am."

Tarpitch, who hated Luther as much as any of the servants, was glad to deliver this news. Blight and Blemish knew what they needed to do and Horton knew he could find Bump in Hercules's Armpit.

However, he didn't have any idea how to get him out.

26

In Which Blight and Blemish Yell “Giddyap” . . .

When Blight and Blemish heard Bump’s message, they panicked for the second time that day.

Simply put, they had no idea where to find Luther. They were so busy looking for Bump, they hadn’t bothered to watch where Luther went after dinner.

Then, in a way that was miraculous and unpleasant at the same time, a voice came to them upon the evening breeze.

“Where are all the boneheaded, foul-smelling, be-spotted stable boys?”

It was Luther!

“Why must we put up with such lazy, brainless, stupid, worthless lollygaggers,” he bellowed. “I’ve been kept waiting for a horse for almost three minutes now! This is what we get for hiring orphans and midgets.”

“Hark!” cried Blight. “Luther must be waiting for assistance in the stables.”

The two boys ran for the stables at full speed.

They arrived to find Luther in full deviltry. Their young master’s face, usually pasty white with a touch of yellow, shone nearly as purple as M’Lady’s Wig Room.

“Where have you been? Why don’t you have a horse ready for me, you lazy hoof-lickers?” he snarled, as Blemish ran to get a saddle and Blight ran to get a horse. “I’ve not time to waste now, but be certain that I will beat you as soon as I have the chance. In the meantime, this will have to do!”

He bopped Blight on the head with a small satchel he was carrying.

Blemish stared in amazement as the satchel popped

open and, for one second, the fading light of early eve shone on its contents—long locks of golden hair. Luther hastily closed the satchel and this time used his fist to clout Blemish on the head.

"Stop gawking, you dungbrain!"

Blemish and Blight finished saddling the horse, and Luther mounted. He kicked the horse hard and galloped down the long drive.

"What destination draws him hence in such a hurry?" asked Blight.

"I do not know, Mr. Blight," said Blemish. "However, wherever he's going he's taking M'Lady Luggertuck's finest wig with him. It was in the bag he hit you with."

"That was a wig, you say? To my estimation, it felt like it weighed at least twenty-three pounds."

"Bump was right! Luther is up to something tonight. We'd better get moving with all due expediency if we wish to follow him."

"Right you are, Mr. Blemish. Shall we saddle Siegfried?"

"So shall it be," said Blemish.

They hurried to saddle Siegfried, the mightiest stallion in the stable. In fact, the mightiest stallion in all the British Isles. A barely tamed creature of furious power and speed.

Blemish said, "Do you know what's quite surprising, Mr. Blight?"

"What's that, Mr. Blemish?"

"I've spent my whole life around these stables, but I've never actually ridden a horse."

"By a curious coincidence the same fact is true of myself, Mr. Blemish," said Blight as he scrambled into the saddle and then pulled Blemish up after him.

"I have, however, often heard the term 'giddyap' used by riders," said Blemish.

"Shall we employ that phrase now, Mr. Blemish?"

"Yes, I should think an advantageous time for its usage has arrived, Mr. Blight."

"Giddyap, Siegfried!" they both shouted, and the horse took off like a cannonball.

Blight and Blemish held on to each other and to the saddle as best they could. Since there seemed to be no means of controlling the fey beast, they could only hope that Siegfried would go in the right direction.

"By M'Lady's Mustache," said one or the other, "this is certainly a bumpy ride!"

27

In Which Miss Neversly's Spoon Is Broken . . .

Talking through the keyhole, Bump and Horton informed each other of the latest developments.

Bump explained how he got stuck and how he had hoped to find the Lump.

"But, Hort, you wouldn't believe what I did find in here!" he said.

"Forks?"

Bump was stunned.

"How on earth did you guess?"

"I didn't guess," said Horton. "Every month, Miss

Neversly brings me down here and makes me polish them all. She wants them to be spotless in case M'Lady Luggertuck ever decides she wants forks again."

"Does that mean that Miss Neversly has a key?"

"Yes! Good thinking!" exclaimed Horton. "But how on earth could I pinch it from her? If I told her the truth, she'd kill us with that spoon of hers."

"Please, Horton, you've got to do something. I'm going to starve to death in here or maybe die of thirst."

"I'll think of something," promised Horton. "First, I'll go get a funnel and a jug and try to pour some water through the keyhole for you. And maybe Loafburton will bake a really, really thin piece of bread for you.

"Then," Horton added, "maybe I can sweet-talk Miss Neversly."

Bump laughed for the first time all day.

Horton ran back to the kitchen, but, before he could find Loafburton or get the funnel or even think about sweet talk, Miss Neversly landed on him like a wolf grabbing a rabbit.

"Guests, guests!" she cried, swinging the spoon wildly. "There are guests coming and all the Garlic-Chip Sherbet Cups are dirty! Dirty! And you, *you,* are off napping as usual! Sloth! Villain! Hugglety-plucker!"

Horton had never seen her so mad. When she calmed down enough to aim her blows a little better, she might really hurt him with that spoon. There was no way he'd be doing any sweet-talking tonight.

"Stop!" came an insistent voice—Loafburton's. Horton saw that the baker's sleeves were wet and soapy.

"Here are your Garlic-Chip Sherbet Cups, Nell," Loafburton snarled, "although I can't imagine any guests will want to eat such a foul dessert. Why can't you make sherbet with raspberries like a decent cook might?"

Miss Neversly forgot all about Horton for the moment, which was just what Loafburton intended. She turned on Loafburton with hate in her heart.

She swung her spoon at the baker. He simply grabbed it in one huge hand and snapped it in two. (Years of kneading bread dough had left the man with extremely powerful arms and hands.)

This was, as everyone in the kitchen knew, a challenge, a thrown-down gauntlet, a slap in the face.

Loafburton had long bristled at following Neversly's commands. Now the Loosening had given him the courage to fight back. But the Loosening hadn't affected Neversly one way or the other—her heart was still as black as her roast beef.

It appeared to all that Neversly and Loafburton would finally battle each other to forever decide who held reign over the kitchen.

Every assistant cook, baker's helper, pastry chef, and coleslaw chopper froze and watched with high hopes of seeing Miss Neversly dethroned. But as Loafburton looked into the cook's eyes, he saw a hateful madness and he knew fear.

Just at that moment, Footman Jennings appeared.

"Horton Halfpott is wanted in the Front Hall," he said.

"What?" snarled Neversly.

"What?" echoed everyone else in the kitchen.

"He's wanted, Cook. Wanted in the Front Hall by one of the guests."

Everyone in the kitchen began whispering and wondering. Who could possibly want to see Horton?

Horton wondered too, of course, but mostly he was

just glad to leave the kitchen. He dodged past the cook and the baker and followed Footman Jennings up the stairs.

Loafburton, relieved, slipped away to check on some dough he had left to rise.

This left Miss Neversly angry and sputtering, but still the empress of the kitchen.

She selected a new spoon from her extensive collection. This one was cast iron and clublike and quite lethal.

28

In Which Celia Saves the Day . . .

When Horton saw that it was Celia Sylvan-Smythe who had asked to see him, he experienced the following sensations:

The rapid percolation of the Halfpott heart, for she was still beautiful and still smiling.

The trembling of the Halfpott stomach, for he knew for certain by now that he really did love her. (Don't worry, this chapter doesn't dwell on that subject.)

A sudden surge of mental cogitation in the Halfpott brain, for suddenly he knew how to rescue Bump.

"Good evening, Mr. Halfpott," called Celia, who was standing in the Front Hall with the Shortleys. They appeared to have just arrived.

Footman Jennings hovered around with their shawls, hats, and canes. A butler stood ready to open the doors to the sitting room, where the Luggertucks were presumably waiting. Several maids were peeping down the stairs. All watched Horton with eager curiosity. This was a rare event indeed—a kitchen boy summoned by a guest. An Unprecedented Marvel.

"I believe, Mr. Halfpott, that you may have dropped this while delivering our invitation some few days ago."

She held out a small package wrapped in brown paper. She had addressed him coldly and formally, but now she gave him a little wink.

"Yes, Miss. Thank you, Miss," Horton said. With all eyes on him, he should be very careful, he knew, yet he said what he needed to say quite boldly:

"While visiting Smugwick Manor, be sure to see the Bejeweled Fork that once belonged to King Henry the Eighth. It is truly one of the family's finest treasures."

Jennings and the butler looked at each other

with raised eyebrows. This babble seemed a little impertinent, but then again it wasn't outright rude. They didn't hear Horton whisper, "Please, Miss, it's important."

That was it. Horton returned to the kitchen (where everybody stared at him) and Celia entered the drawing room (where everybody, especially Montgomery, stared at her).

"Oh, Celia," gushed M'Lady Luggertuck, "I'm so sorry that my son, Luther, isn't here to receive you. I don't know where he's gotten to. However, here is Montgomery, who has been so eager to see you."

"Would you like to walk in the garden?" Montgomery slobbered.

Desperate to avoid this fate, Celia said, "M'Lady Luggertuck, I've been told that you own King Henry the Eighth's Bejeweled Fork. I would so love to see it. I've always been particularly fascinated with Royal Silverware." (This was a white lie. Celia didn't give a huggletypluck for anybody's silverware.)

M'Lady Luggertuck bristled at the mention of the word "fork." However, since Celia was a guest in her home and since it was a chance to show off the family's wealth, she called out: "Jennings, have Miss Neversly send up the Bejeweled Fork."

Jennings made another trip to the kitchen and asked Miss Neversly for the fork.

Neversly, who kept the key on a chain around her neck, pulled the chain off, threw the heavy iron key at Horton's head, and snarled:

"Go fetch the fork, boy, and it better be spotless or I'll . . ."

Horton didn't wait to hear the rest. He grabbed the key and ran for the Vestibule of Large Roman Objects.

Thus was Bump freed!

Celia, for her part, was not free. She was forced to feign interest in what is perhaps the ugliest fork ever made and then eat some nasty-tasting sherbet and then listen to M'Lady Luggertuck yammer on and on, all the while trying to avoid Montgomery.

During the long ride home she puzzled over why Horton had wanted her to see the fork. But she smiled when she thought of him opening her present: a small leather-bound book entitled *The Flora and Fauna of British Mires, Moors, Bogs, and Large Puddles*. On the frontispiece of which she had penciled, "This may be useful the next time you come to visit me, which I hope will be soon. Your friend, Celia." Reader, you may well imagine what effect these words had worked on Horton.

29

In Which Two Wigs Are Worse Than One . . .

Siegfried flung himself with reckless disregard for his passengers, Blight and Blemish, down the road to the village, Lugger-Upon-the-Wold. Luckily, this is where Luther had gone, too, and—again, luckily—the two boys didn't fall off.

Because of Siegfried's speed and daring, they arrived in the village just a minute after Luther.

However, in the growing darkness, they might never have seen him if not for the wig, which Luther now wore as he entered Slaughterboard's Inn.

“That was a surprising sight,” said Blemish.

“I must concur,” said Blight. “Mr. Blemish, would you care to join me in peeking in the window of this establishment to see if we may determine the reason for the surprising sight?”

“As you wish, Mr. Blight.”

They dismounted, or rather fell, from Siegfried—who had slowed down a bit to inspect the village’s population of lady horses—and proceeded to peek into the window, which stood open due to the warm weather.

Blight and Blemish, who were perspiring due to the warm weather, ducked back down immediately. Luther, wearing not just the wig but also Colonel Sitwell’s monocle, sat at a table just a few feet away.

Luther hadn’t seen them. His attention was fixed on someone else seated at the table—incredibly it was another man wearing a wig and a monocle!

“Did you, Mr. Blemish, see not one, but two bewigged men?” whispered Blight.

“Yes,” whispered Blemish. “Yes, I did. Did you recognize the other bewigged man, Mr. Blight?”

“Regrettably, no.”

But you, Reader, would have recognized the man.

So would Horton. For it was none other than Captain Splinterlock, leader of the Shipless Pirates. Ah, how differently things would have worked out if they had but known who the man was.

They strained their ears as best they could and heard this conversation:

"Smedlap, I presume?"

"Yes," said Luther, "I am Monsieur Smedlap and you must be—"

"Hush!" hissed the mystery man. "My name is known to every constable, judge, and hangman from here to Cape Horn!"

"Oh, sorry."

"I must congratulate you, young man, on the high quality of your disguise. Not only do the long locks of hair conceal your identity, but they are also very Fashionable."

The mystery man continued. "Well, Mr. Smedlap, I received your letter—which showed very sloppy penmanship and spelling by the way—and I've come a long way to meet you here tonight. I hope it will be worth my while."

"Yes," said Luther, "it certainly will be. Your task is simple. Your reward great!"

The stable boys' eyes grew wider and wider as they listened to Luther begin the most outrageous string of bald-faced lies they had ever heard:

"Tomorrow night at Smugwick Manor there will be a costume ball. A noted traitor to the Queen will be there."

"Traitor?" said the mystery man, sounding doubtful.

"Yes," said Luther. "She will be dressed as Little Bo-peep."

"Bo-peep?" said the mystery man, sounding even more doubtful.

"I need you and your men to kidnap her, since she cannot be arrested for various important but top-secret reasons."

"Top-secret reasons?" said the mystery man, sounding so doubtful that Luther began to squirm uncomfortably and scratch under his wig. "Are you certain that this is an honorable task?"

"Er, yes?" said Luther.

"It had better be," said the mystery man, "or I'll have the honor of making you walk the plank." The mystery man laughed. The deep, ugly rumble covered Blemish's and Blight's arms with goose bumps. Luther's, too.

"Now," said the mystery man, "do you have what you promised in your letter? Do you have the Lump?"

"Yes, I have it."

"Let me see it!"

"Not here, but somewhere no one else could ever find it. I'll give it to you right after the ball tomorrow night."

"You'd better, boy, you'd better!"

Luther scratched under his wig again.

"I did want to add just one thing," said Luther. "There's a kitchen boy who's been causing some trouble. I thought maybe you could—"

"No," said the mystery man. "Kitchen boys cost extra. A lot extra. They often turn out to be plucky little heroes with hearts of gold and a grim determination to see justice done."

"Oh, forget it then," growled Luther, who felt he was already paying too much. "I'll take care of him myself."

Blemish and Blight looked at each other in horror.

"Luther's after Horton!" whispered Blemish.

"This calls for all due expediency!" whispered Blight.

They ran back to Siegfried, clambered on, and shouted "Giddyap!" The mighty stallion, sensing their urgency, gave a wild snort, shook his flowing mane, and hurtled off in the wrong direction.

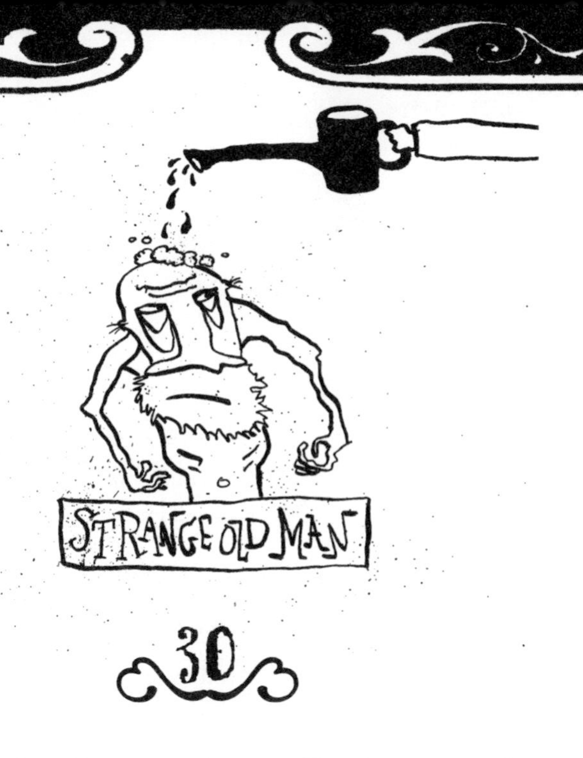

30

In Which Horton Gets Ready for the Ball . . .

All the servants were up late, getting everything just as M'Lady Luggertuck wanted it.

The banisters were burnished. The rug fringes were combed. The strange old man who lived inside the Leftmost Turret was bathed. (An Unprecedented Marvel, by the way.)

One by one the servants finished their tasks and went to bed. Soon Horton stood alone at his sink. Finally, as the grouchy kitchen clock clonked twelve times, he finished polishing the last piece of the Luggertuck Silver—an enormous cheese platter as long as a tall man and as wide as a fat one.

Tiredness nagged at his eyes and a numbness grabbed at his brain. But he could not go to bed yet.

For Horton had a plan, too. He meant to make good on his whispered words to Celia. He meant to go to the ball.

Yes, yes, he knew that he would have to bend the rules a bit here, since he didn't have an invitation and, in fact, would be totally unwelcome in every way conceivable.

But Horton was undergoing a Loosening of his own. He had already broken several rules—talking to Celia, searching for Bump, tricking Neversly out of the key—and he regretted it not at all.

Perhaps, he began to realize, not every preposterous pronouncement of M'Lady Luggertuck needed to be obeyed. Nor every tyrannical decree of Miss Neversly. Nor every unwritten law of propriety that prevented kitchen boys from befriending young ladies.

Anyway, what did he need with an invitation? He was already inside the manor, after all. The only thing he needed was a costume that made him totally unrecognizable.

And he knew just where to find it.

He lit a candle, climbed the stairs, and turned the glass doorknob of Lord Emberly's study.

It was empty. He had hoped the kindly old man would be there. But since he wasn't, Horton decided he would borrow what he needed anyway. Surely Lord Emberly would not mind.

Horton used his candle stump to light Lord Emberly's fancy monkey lamp.

Then he dug through the trunk. Yes, just as he remembered—an ornate Oriental costume with a grinning white mask. It had been a gift to Lord Emberly from a certain lovely young actress in the Mount Fuji Theatrical Company. Bittersweet thoughts of this young actress still danced through Lord Emberly's memories, but that was one story he had not chosen to share with Horton.

Horton wrapped the silk robes around the mask and carefully tucked it all under his grubby jacket.

He left the room, went upstairs to the attic, and hid the costume under the flimsy mattress on his cot.

This made sleeping even less comfortable than usual, but he didn't care. He was too excited. He would see Celia the next day. He went to sleep happy, which was quite rare.

How sad, then, to have to tell you that at the very moment that Horton was searching the trunk, Luther Luggertuck was returning from his meeting with Splinterlock in the village.

Luther saw the window of Lord Emberly's study aglow with the light of the monkey lamp.

"That's odd," he thought. "I thought I was the only one who went sneaking around where I don't belong in the middle of the night."

He decided to investigate. He arrived just in time to peep through the keyhole—there certainly is a lot of keyhole peeping in this story, isn't there, Reader?—to see Horton taking the gown and mask.

Then he hid in the shadows as Horton left the room and carried the costume up to the servants' attic.

"I'm certainly glad I didn't pay that pirate to get rid of the kitchen boy," Luther thought to himself, giddy with black joy. "I'll let that fat detective do it for me for free."

31

In Which Lies Are Told . . .

The next morning—the dawn of the day of the ball—Portnoy St. Pomfrey was just lifting the sweet golden goodness of his fifth anchovy-stuffed deviled egg to his lips when Luther burst into the breakfast room.

"Mr. St. Pomfrey! The thief has struck again!"

St. Pomfrey jumped in his chair and dropped another eggy bit onto his suit. His nerves were as tight as harpsichord strings, and Luther's announcement hit a ringy, keyless chord.

For the first time in his career, St. Pomfrey felt

unsure of his abilities. Things kept getting stolen and he was making no progress, though he frequently told the Luggertucks the opposite.

Sir, M'Lady, Montgomery, and the colonel, who were also seated at the table, jumped, too.

"Oh no, not my collection of Pewter Chickens!" shrieked M'Lady Luggertuck.

Luther was momentarily taken aback by this. He hadn't been prepared for such a stupid statement, even from his mother. Even he wouldn't bother stealing those stupid chickens.

"No! Much worse, Mother. My costume. My costume for the ball. My beautiful Oriental gown that I ordered from London at great expense."

Are we surprised, Reader, that he stood there and lied and pretended to cry? No, we are not.

"Are there any clues, motives, footprints, ink stains, paint smears, or paper trails?" inquired St. Pomfrey hopefully, even desperately.

"Only that a footman saw one of the kitchen boys in the hall near my room," lied Luther.

"Aha!" shouted St. Pomfrey.

"But surely you don't think that a kitchen boy would

have stolen it and hidden it up in the servants' quarters, do you?" asked Luther, with a syrupy tone that he had learned from listening to his mother talk to his father.

"That's exactly what I think!" cried St. Pomfrey.

"Brilliant detective work," cheered Luther.

"The case is solved!" cried M'Lady Luggertuck. She jumped up and pulled the nearest silver rope with a gold tassel.

Footman Jennings arrived a moment later.

"Jennings, send for Constable Wholecloth immediately."

Jennings was dying to ask why the constable was needed, but he only said, "Yes, M'Lady."

As soon as he left the room, St. Pomfrey spoke again.

"I fear we may be too late if we wait for the constable to arrive. The thief could even now be destroying the evidence. We must search the servants' quarters immediately! We have no time to lose!"

(Actually he found time to grab several muffins and a smoked kipper, but he did move quickly for the first time since his arrival.)

Not trusting any of the servants, they all ran up the stairs to the attic to see for themselves. Perhaps "ran" is not an apt description of the way M'Lady huffed and puffed, clutched her heart, sagged, drooped, fainted, and was eventually pushed from behind by Sir Luggertuck and St. Pomfrey.

None of the Luggertucks had ever actually been to the servants' attic before. M'Lady Luggertuck looked around at the unpainted walls, the leaky roof, and the rusty cots and sniffed. "Oh, those servants have such abominable taste."

They found the costume under Horton's mattress, of course, but not the Lump or any of the other missing things. However, Portnoy St. Pomfrey declared it safe to assume that Horton had stolen the Lump as well, but had hidden it more carefully.

"Let's go ask him where," said St. Pomfrey, eagerly anticipating his reward.

"Yes!" agreed Luther Luggertuck, eagerly anticipating the arrest of Horton.

"Yes!" agreed M'Lady Luggertuck, eagerly anticipating firing Horton.

"Yes!" agreed Montgomery, eagerly saying what everyone else said.

32

In Which Horton Runs Like a Rabbit with Foxes Close Behind . . .

With M'Lady Luggertuck leading the way, the group stormed down the stairs and into the kitchen.

Yet another Unprecedented Marvel—M'Lady Luggertuck in the kitchen.

Miss Neversly blushed and began a deep curtsy—this was her great dream, a visit from M'Lady! Perhaps, after all these years, M'Lady was finally going to offer one tiny compliment or word of thanks.

But M'Lady, red with anger, brushed the cook aside.

Loosened corset or no, M'Lady felt the fiery pleasure of a good tantrum brewing deep in her fashionable gut. Bile surged through her veins. (She hadn't been this worked up since the incident with the pigeon in "The Ruination of M'Lady Luggertuck's Favorite Hat.")

"Where's that filthy kitchen boy?"

The heads of five filthy kitchen boys popped up—all round-eyed with fear.

"That's the one there," hollered Luther, pointing at Horton. *"J'accuse!"*

"Where's the Lump?" shouted several people at once, rushing toward Horton's sink.

"We found the costume you stole," snarled Luther. "Now, where's the rest?"

Horton wasn't sure what was going on, but it was clear that it would end badly.

In a blink, he was gone. Montgomery, who had been blinking, thought that Horton actually vanished, but the rest saw a feat that they would remember forever.

Horton dove headfirst between Sir Luggertuck and St. Pomfrey. Sliding on the wet floor, he swished under the kipper-carving table, hooked an arm around a table leg, skidded off at an angle, rolled, sprang to his feet, leapt to a chair, then to the cheese slicing table, then to a sideboard, then to the top of a China cupboard.

Finally, using the surprised, but rubbery, head of Miss Neversly as a springboard, he leapt toward a hanging lantern, grabbed it, and swung toward a grease-spattered window.

Alas, the window was closed! Things looked bleak!

But remember, Reader, that Horton was a nice young fellow and had made many friends among the servants.

It pays to be nice. Maybe not right away, but someday. For Horton, that day had arrived.

The baker, Loafburton, with one quick motion of his powerful, flour-covered arm, yanked the window open just in time and Horton shot through.

Miss Neversly threw her spoon after him but 'twas too late. Horton tucked, rolled, and came up running.

Most everyone froze with astonishment, but, unfortunately, Portnoy St. Pomfrey froze not. He was a professional criminologist, after all.

The big detective strode to the window, opened his enormous jowly mouth, and bellowed: "Hillhemp!

Gateberry! Howbag! Gentlemen and Lady of the Press! There goes your story! There goes the thief! The kitchen boy did it!"

Hillhemp, Gateberry, and Howbag, who had been sulking around the front door for the past week, suddenly snapped their heads up, narrowed their eyes, tensed their muscles, and began composing headlines.

COLD-BLOODED KITCHEN BOY CAUGHT!

DISHWASHER DOES DIRTY DIAMOND DEED!

ANOTHER TRIUMPH FOR PORTNOY ST. POMFREY!

Horton was running right toward them. He tried to reverse his direction, but it was too late.

They lunged, they swarmed, they plucked at his shirtsleeves.

"Care to comment, kitchen boy?"

"What made you do it?"

"How do you spell your last name?"

Horton Halfpott was, indeed, caught.

33

In Which Horton Is on the Hook . . .

Portnoy St. Pomfrey strutted and boasted. He piled fib on top of lie on top of exaggeration and cemented it all with hyperbole. The reporters wrote it all down.

Miss Neversly alternated between hitting Horton with her biggest cast-iron spoon and demanding, "Where's the Lump?"

M'Lady Luggertuck reveled in a state of ecstatic maliciousness.

Luther smiled. Once, when no one else could hear, he whispered in Horton's ear.

I can't bear to tell you what he said. But I guess you must know, mustn't you? All right, if you must know:

Luther said, "I don't guess Miss Celia Sylvan-Smythe will be quite so sweet after she finds out you're a little thief. Or perhaps I should call her the future Mrs. Luther Luggertuck!"

Horton said nothing. At least part of what Luther said was true, he realized. Whatever feelings she might have had for him would be crushed. However, he felt sure that she would never become the future Mrs. Luther Luggertuck. At least, he prayed that she would not.

Could any words have saved the situation, he would have said them. But no poet, no orator, no ballyhooer, and certainly no kitchen boy could have turned this tide with mere words.

Even if he broke his promise and told everyone about Lord Emberly and the study, no one would believe him. Anyway, he realized, he didn't have permission from Lord Emberly to take the costume.

So Horton said nothing.

At last, Jennings returned with Constable Wholecloth.

"Ah, the smelly, muddy one. I knew it all along!" cried

the constable, rudely, upon arrival. "He probably hid it in the mire. It'll never be found until he tells us where to look."

"Oh, no!" cried M'Lady Luggertuck.

"Don't worry, ma'am; one night in my jail and he'll be ready to talk. We've got a full house of prisoners right now. Real mean ones and just as smelly as this runty kitchen boy."

Horton's arms and legs were tied and he was put in a little wagon, which Constable Wholecloth drove back to town.

As they passed the stables, Horton saw Bump waving to him. Bump was very worried because Blight and Blemish hadn't returned and now Horton was being hauled away. However, he still tried to raise Horton's spirits.

"Don't worry, Hort!" Bump called. "We'll get you out!"

Horton called good-bye to his friend, but, in truth, he didn't think he stood much chance of escaping.

Besides, any tiny, feeble hope that he might win the heart of Miss Celia Sylvan-Smythe seemed to have disappeared. And that felt even worse than being in trouble.

34

In Which a Shot Rings Out . . .

By the time Blight and Blemish figured out how to steer Siegfried, they were a long way away.

It was morning when they finally got back to Lugger-Upon-the-Wold and started down the road to Smugwick Manor. Siegfried was no longer in any hurry. The stable boys, however, were.

"Won't our noble steed go any faster, Mr. Blight? We've got to get back and warn Horton."

"Well, Mr. Blemish, I have said giddyap many times,

but he still isn't giddy," answered Blight. "Perhaps the creature is tiring."

Then they saw a wagon approaching. It was driven by Constable Wholecloth and there in the back sat their good friend Horton Halfpott. Tied up!

"Ah, here he is now," said Blemish. He began to call loudly.

"Mr. Halfpott! Mr. Halfpott! We regret that we have disturbing news to deliver. Luther is planning to cause you harm!"

"Thank you, Blemish," answered Horton. "I've found out the hard way."

"Oh dear, I can see that," called Blemish. "May we be of any assistance?"

"No, you may not!" roared Constable Wholecloth, stopping his wagon and drawing his pistol. "Get away from my prisoner."

"He seems rather rude, Mr. Blight," said Blemish.

"Yes, he does," said Blight. "However, I fear we must risk agitating him further. We have additional information to impart."

"I agree," said Blemish, and he called out again.

“Mr. Halfpott, Luther has hired some men to kidnap someone at the ball tonight.”

“Who?” asked Horton.

“Silence!” shouted Constable Wholecloth, and he rudely fired his pistol into the air.

The gunshot startled Siegfried and the mighty stallion began to gallop down the road with renewed vigor. (The constable’s horse stayed put. He had grown accustomed to gunshots, shouting, and rudeness.)

“Who?” cried Horton again.

Blemish, just barely hanging on to Blight, who was just barely hanging on to the saddle, called over his shoulder.

“Little Bo-peep!”

And with that, Siegfried, Blight, and Blemish were around a bend and out of sight.

Suddenly Horton cared very much about escaping.

35

In Which St. Pomfrey Weighs the Evidence . . .

Blemish and Blight arrived back at the stables and quickly held a conference with Bump.

"The best way to prove that Horton is not the thief is to prove that Luther is," said Bump. "We've collected the evidence. Now it's time to go see Portnoy St. Pomfrey."

Normally, it would have been difficult for three stable boys to enter the respectable parts of the manor.

But today was the day of the ball and the entire edifice swarmed with servants carrying out M'Lady Luggertuck's last-minute orders.

She stomped around the house inspecting and belittling the servants' work. This was not an Unprecedented Marvel. In fact, it was a fairly common occurrence. (See "The White Glove of M'Lady Luggertuck.") Even with her corset Loosened, M'Lady was a bully of the worst sort.

"These throw rugs were not thrown properly!" she bellowed. "These drapes are not draped properly! These French doors are not French enough!"

Bump, Blight, and Blemish each picked up a chair and pretended they were moving them. Luckily, no one thought to ask why three chairs were needed in Portnoy St. Pomfrey's room.

They found the detective making out his bill. His mood ran as high as the grand total he tallied up. He would be charging the Luggertucks a lot of money as soon as his suspect, Horton, broke down and told them where the Lump was hidden.

"Ah, Bump, I see you have brought a couple of your equally equiney friends with you!" St. Pomfrey cried merrily. "Well, you didn't bring me many Valuable Clues, but I'll let you all share in the reward anyway."

He gave each of them a tarnished penny.

"Don't worry, I'll just add it to the bill," he chortled. "And here, help yourself to some Caramel Anchovy Brickle."

"No, Mr. St. Pomfrey," said Bump. "We didn't come for a reward. We came to tell you who stole the Lump."

"Too late! I personally apprehended the vile culprit just a few hours ago after a brutally dangerous struggle that required all of my strength and several jujitsu moves to—"

Bump interrupted.

"We don't have time for all that. Luther plans to strike tonight."

"Luther?" asked Portnoy St. Pomfrey. "You mean the old guy with the monocle?"

"No, that's Colonel Sitwell. Haven't you been paying attention at all?" shouted Bump, whose ears were turning red. "Luther is M'Lady's son!"

"Ah, yes, such a fine young gentleman."

Bump's ears were sizzling. He was a nice little fellow, but this was too much. Though he didn't know it—and, alas, won't find out during the course of this book—royal blood ran in his veins. When called upon, the tiny stable boy could face down anyone, even a gargantuan detective. He prepared to launch an angry barrage of insults that would have included the words "lazy," "idiot," and "halitosis."

"Ahem," said Blight, clamping his hand over Bump's mouth. "Perhaps Mr. Bump would allow us to interject."

"Begging your pardon, sir," said Blemish to the detective, "your zealous pursuit of justice has no doubt been so relentless that you had no chance to observe the following facts."

Blemish told him about seeing Luther replace the bust of Napoleon.

Blight described seeing Luther wearing the wig and the monocle.

Blemish, speaking for Bump, showed him the stolen stationery found in the Fork Vault, which had been opened with Crotty's keys.

Finally, Blight revealed how they had overheard Luther's plan to use the Lump to pay the kidnappers.

St. Portnoy was impressed. The boys had certainly put forth a lot more effort than he had.

"That, my sagacious stable boys, is a fine theory. Cultivated with a wit as sharp as the odor that clings to your bestained breeches. I congratulate myself on seeing within you the potential for impressive powers of deduction and detection."

Bump, Blight, and Blemish had little idea what he was talking about. But it appeared that he believed them.

"Howsoever," the detective continued, "deduction and detection are deficient without discovery. Until you have found the Lump, your theory is nothing more than a theory. I cannot accuse Luther Luggertuck, son of the wealthiest family in the area—and the family that is paying my enormous fee—without proof. You must find the Lump first!"

"That shall be no problem," said Bump. "I know exactly where it is."

"You do?" thundered St. Pomfrey.

"You do?" asked Blight.

"Muwr Gnu?" asked Blemish, whose mouth was full of Caramel Anchovy Brickle.

Yes, Reader, he did. The question is: Do you?

36

In Which Piracy Plays a Hand . . .

By the time Horton was hauled into Lugger-Upon-the-Wold, berated by various town officials, questioned by the magistrate, and taken to jail, it was early evening.

Horton knew that all across the county, 'folks were getting ready for the big costume ball.

It seemed possible that he would spend long years in jail, but all he could think about was Bump and Blight's message: Luther was out to kidnap Celia.

Even as he was being dragged down a filthy set of stairs toward the town's small, but unpleasant, dungeon, he was trying to figure out how he could escape and warn her.

Suddenly he smelled fish. Old fish.

The constable, rudely dragging him by the ear, opened a cell door and threw him in, once again rudely. (Why must he be so rude, Reader?)

It was very dark inside. There were no windows and no candles. Horton tripped and fell on the floor, which was an inch deep with filth.

"'Ere's a new friend for you. Maybe 'e'll join your crew," the constable said, and laughed and laughed as he barred the door.

"Stow it, you fat tub of whale blubber, or you'll find yourself walking the plank," shouted someone inside the dark cell.

Constable Wholecloth just laughed harder at this.

"You lot don't even have a plank!" he called, and stomped off.

"He's right, Cap'n, we don't have a plank," said someone, and there began a lot of grumbling.

"Hush, boys, we'll get our plank and a new ship to go with it, once we finish tonight's job."

"But how can we do the job when we're stuck in jail?"

“’Tis a good point, Bart. A good point. It’s so dark in here I couldn’t see a mermaid’s—”

Horton interrupted, “I’ve got some candles, sir.”

“Who’s that? The new prisoner?”

“Yes, sir, it’s me, Horton Halfpott, the fellow with the leg of lamb.”

“Good to see you again, boy, though I can’t actually see you. Do you mean to lend us your candles and help us escape?”

“Certainly,” said Horton, pulling several of his precious candle stubs from his pockets. “But I don’t have any way to light them.”

“Don’t worry, son, Old Bart’s pipe ain’t never gone out, not in typhoon nor gale nor belly of whale.”

Old Bart held the candles one by one to the glowing tobaccy in his pipe. Soon the cell was dimly lit by four flickering candle stubs.

“Look at the rust on those bars,” said a patch-eyed pirate named Lawrence.

“Why are you in jail?” Horton asked, again against his and my better judgment.

“Argh,” muttered Captain Splinterlock, “a small

disagreement over the price of food and lodging at Slaughterboard's Inn."

"Cap'n!" called Lawrence. "Look!"

Old Bart, grinning ear to ear, held a rusty bar that he'd yanked barehanded out of the door.

"Great, pull out a couple more bars and we'll be on our way," ordered the captain.

Old Bart put down his anchor, grabbed two bars, and gave a mighty heave, then a disappointed groan.

"Sorry, Cap'n."

"Maybe someone could wiggle out," suggested Lawrence.

"Nay, none of us are that skinny."

"I am, sir," said Horton. They all looked at him. Yes, malnourished as he was from eating gruel, he might just make it.

"You won't leave us, will you, old boy? You will open the door for us," the captain said, as if they were old shipmates who'd been round the Horn and back again. "We've got important work tonight, catching a traitor."

"Yes, sir," said Horton, and holding his breath he

slowly wiggled and squirmed through the small gap. It took about five minutes and it hurt.

When at last he slipped through, he unbarred the door and the pirates swarmed out.

The captain shook his hand.

"Good work, lad. I'll be sure that you get credit when we capture the traitor."

"Who is the traitor?" asked Horton, feeling pretty good about himself.

"We don't know," admitted the captain. "All we know is that she'll be at the Luggertucks' costume ball tonight—dressed as Little Bo-peep."

"Oh no!" cried Horton, feeling pretty bad about himself.

"Let's go, boys, we're late," cried the captain, running out the door with his crew behind him.

At that moment, the constable, who had obviously been napping, came running down the hall, but Old Bart conked him on the head with the rusty steel bar.

"Wait!" called Horton. "Not Little Bo-peep. She's not a traitor! She's—"

Old Bart turned around. "We almost forgot," he said with a grin. He picked Horton up with one hand

and threw him back into the cell and rebarred the door. "Be good, boy."

Horton hollered after them, but nary a pirate listened.

Minutes later, after Horton had again squirmed through the bars, the pirates were long gone.

He ran outside, where a farmer was shouting that smelly ruffians had stolen his horse and wagon.

Now Horton understood Luther's plan, or at least the major points of it, and he understood that it would have failed if he hadn't helped the pirates get out of jail.

37

In Which M'Lady Luggertuck Stinks . . .

Much has been said, Reader, about the odors of our hardworking stable boys, of our fish-reeking pirates, of our sardine-eating detective, and even of our mire-slogging hero.

But what of M'Lady Luggertuck's odor?

As odors go, it was an expensive one, bottled in Paris. (Or at least the perfume clerks assured her the bottles were from Paris.)

As she prepared to be the grand hostess of her grand

ball, M'Lady Luggertuck had carefully contemplated how she might dress most grandly.

Two great burdens weighed on her mind.

Burden the First: Her finest Fashionable Wig was still missing. (Luther had chucked it in a ditch on his way back from his secret meeting.)

Burden the Second: Her corset was still Loosened. This meant she would appear perhaps a tad heavy, but she just wasn't prepared to tighten it again. Not yet, at least.

Unlike her son, M'Lady Luggertuck still had a seed of decency a'dwelling deep inside. Since Loosening the corset, she had felt the seed stir, ready to shoot out roots of common goodness and petals of human charity.

Perhaps there remained hope for the lady yet. Perhaps she might become a cheerful, forgiving, and helpful person, content with her lot in life. She decided to leave her corset untightened lest tightening it should smother the seedling.

How, then, could she rise above these fashion challenges? With more perfume, of course!

After several days of consideration, she chose "Eau d'Peccary" over "Congealed Ambrosia." Partially because "Eau d'Peccary" gave off a foresty air that she felt would enhance her costume. (She planned to dress as a wood nymph.) And partially because Old Crotty found two big jugs of "Eau d'Peccary" in a closet.

Shortly before the ball was to begin, Old Crotty, who blessedly had lost her sense of smell from repeated exposure to M'Lady's perfumes, began to slather M'Lady Luggertuck with the syrupy scent.

The thick stone walls of Smugwick Manor once, long ago, held up against an assault by Belgian Crusaders, but they were no match for "Eau d'Peccary," which stormed the old castle like a berserker. No one, except Old Crotty, was safe.

Stable boys shoveling manure wrinkled their noses. Loafburton, tasting the Royal Rum Plum Rumpus he had baked for the ball, made a gagging noise and threw out the whole batch. Colonel Sitwell, napping in a hammock some fifty yards from the manor, awoke screaming, "Rally, men! The natives are attacking!"

Yes, men, do rally! For M'Lady Luggertuck is ready for a party.

38

In Which Luther Sees His Plan Go Perfectly . . .

M'Lady Luggertuck entered the ballroom to be greeted by a surging tide of fawning compliments from the Invited Guests.

Her costume was so very lovely. Her wig so very fashionable. And the ballroom so very shiny and glittery.

Of course, the Invited Guests should have complimented the servants who had shined it and glittered it. But they did not do that; nor did they even speak to the servants, except to say "more this," "more that," and "go away."

The Invited Guests thought everything so very perfect, except for the horrendous stench of M'Lady Luggertuck's perfume, "Eau d'Peccary." (If only she had looked "peccary" up in the dictionary!)

About midway through the ball, the smell actually became worse—an Unprecedented Marvel—when her perfume began to mingle with a strange smell of old fish in the air. Most Invited Guests attributed this to Colonel Sitwell.

Otherwise, what a lovely affair, Reader! So many wealthy people wearing costumes ordered from the finest costumiers in London. Lady Aiken was dressed as a wolf. Lord Alexander was dressed as Puss in Boots. The Empress of Blandings was dressed as a well-groomed pig.

The Shortleys, dressed as Robin Hood and Maid Marian, brought Celia Sylvan-Smythe, dressed, as promised, as Little Bo-peep.

The local elite were there: the Frimperton family (gnomes), Reverend Apoplexy (King Lear) and his daughters (King Lear's daughters), and the esteemed

Dr. Radish and his wife (St. George and, fittingly, a dragon.)

Colonel Sitwell and Montgomery were dressed as Colonel Sitwell and Montgomery.

And, of course, the two dozen suitors were all dressed as Romeo, even the seventy-three-year-old one. They pressed close to our Miss Sylvan-Smythe. They begged for dances, but she declined, at first politely and finally quite brashly. Still, they fawned over her and brought her more punch than she could possibly drink.

Luther Luggertuck did not bother. Why jostle with the crowd when he, alone, had planned ahead? He'd have plenty of time to talk to Celia after the kidnapping.

Always egregious at parties, Luther behaved abominably again this time, but in a quieter way than usual. He was, after all, in disguise, wearing the Oriental robes and the creepy grinning mask.

He hung around the smorgasbord all evening, stuffing Sweet Sugarapple Pie into his gaping maw. What a relief that the mask hid his bad habit of chewing with his mouth open!

Eventually he sauntered over to a group of guests dressed as pirates. These pirates wore amazingly good costumes. Scars, tattoos, wooden legs, fleas—very authentic-looking!

Had anyone—say, three stable boys and a massive detective hiding under a table—eavesdropped, this is what they would have heard:

"I'm Monsieur Smedlap," Luther said to the captain.

"Aye," replied Captain Splinterlock, "and I'm an innocent guest dressed as Captain Obediah Splinterlock, terror of the Tortugas and handsomest man on the high seas!"

Luther rolled his eyes. Luckily for him the mask hid this, or Captain Splinterlock would have flogged him.

"It's a quarter of ten now," he told the captain. "At ten o'clock the big grandfather clock will begin striking. That will be your signal. Grab Little Bo-peep and go out the French doors into the garden."

"I don't see no French doors," said Old Bart.

"Right there," said Luther impatiently, pointing at the doors.

"They don't look very French to me," said Lawrence, the patch-eyed pirate.

"Never mind," snapped Luther. "Go out the not-very-French doors into the garden. Follow the path through the woods and meet me by the edge of the mire."

"And you'll be getting us our Lump?" demanded the captain.

"Yes, yes, as soon as I see you get the girl, I'll run and get it from its hiding place."

"You'd better bring it or, by the drowned timbers of our old ship, I'll make you walk the plank."

"But Cap'n, we don't have a—"

"Hush!" roared the captain. Several guests looked over.

"You're attracting too much attention," hissed Luther. "Disperse!"

"Gladly," said Old Bart, and charted a course for the ale. Lawrence headed for a buffet of fine cheeses.

Meanwhile, the captain actually asked M'Lady Luggertuck for a dance.

"Such a dancer! Such a man!" thought M'Lady Luggertuck. "If only Sir Luggertuck could move this way." Had she known such a handsome man would be at the ball, she might have tightened her corset.

Luther felt he should be as far from Miss Sylvan-Smythe as possible, in case something went wrong. He stood near the musicians and jokingly waved his hands as if he were a conductor. The musicians glowered.

Ten o'clock neared. Luther's chest a'tightened with a moment of worry. He didn't see Miss Sylvan-Smythe anywhere. Where had she gotten to?

The clock began to strike ten!

The ballroom was crowded. He looked around. No Little Bo-peep. His stomach a'bubbled with angry acid.

Then, relief. There, across the giant room, near the cheeses, he saw her elaborately frilled bonnet. Suddenly pirates surrounded her. They put a sack over her head and, moving as a large clump, headed for the (French) doorway.

Montgomery remarked that the guests dressed as pirates were ill-mannered, but certainly had jolly good costumes. A moment later the pirates were through the doors and into the garden.

I refuse to describe the smile on Luther's face as he congratulated himself on a perfect plan.

"And now to fetch the Lump and have a little chat with Miss Sylvan-Smythe. We should be announcing our engagement by midnight," he murmured.

39

In Which We Learn What Luther Did Not See . . .

Reader, do not panic. Do not throw the book down in anger. Do not wonder how Horton could have failed, because, of course, he did not.

What Luther saw was not all there was to see. If we are to see it, we must turn back the clock a little. We must revisit the recent past, just a half hour before the kidnapping.

What was happening then? Horton was stumbling

over rocks and roots on the shortcut from town in a Headlong Rush to get to Smugwick Manor.

Finally he emerged from Wolfleg Woods to see the castle aglow with lights. But it looked not beautiful, not to him.

Nearly exhausted, he ran onward to the stable. The various garden and stable boys cheered when they saw him.

"You escaped, eh?"

"Hurrah, Horton! Well done."

"Did you come back for the Lump? Where'd you hide it?"

"No time, no time," gasped Horton, huffing and puffing after his long run. "Where's Bump? Where's Blight and Blemish?"

"Haven't seen them in hours."

"Please, you have to help me; I have to get into the ball. I need a costume."

Tarpitch, the oldest stable boy, opened the tack-room door. "Why not take one of Luther's riding suits and a helmet?"

"Perfect," Horton said. Then, inspiration struck. "In fact, I'll take two of each."

Donning one coat and one helmet, he tucked the others inside the coat and headed for the servants' entrance. Before he got there he saw, standing on a terrace with her back to the great ballroom, a beautiful shepherdess: Little Bo-peep.

He dove into the bushes at the foot of the terrace.

"Miss Sylvan-Smythe! Miss Sylvan-Smythe!" he whispered loudly.

She looked over the edge of the terrace and lit up with joy, a real smile on her face for the first time that night.

"Mr. Halfpott, is that you? You came after all!"

"Are you alone?"

"For the moment, thank goodness. I snuck out. There are so many . . . er, suitors, in there."

Looking up, he saw again how beautiful she was, despite the frills and ribbons of the silly costume.

"You're beautiful," he said, not against his better judgment or mine either. "But you have to change costumes. There are worse men than suitors at the ball. Luther Luggertuck has hired pirates to kidnap you."

Some girls might have screamed. Others would have laughed and called him silly. Celia nodded.

“I’m not one bit surprised. He is a vile young man,” she said. “But what good will it do to change costumes?”

“The pirates are looking for Little Bo-peep. As long as you’re wearing that costume you’re in danger. I’ve brought you another.”

“Good, I’ve gotten tired of being Little Bo-peep anyway. Too frilly,” said Celia. Then she laughed. “But I can’t change here, in front of you.”

Horton blushed.

It was decided that she would change behind a bush, with Horton standing guard—and looking the other way, I hardly need mention.

The Little Bo-peep costume was not easy to squirm out of, especially when one was hiding in a bush, but, as has been hinted at previously, Celia Sylvan-Smythe did not balk easily. As she struggled out of the dress with its many bows and buttons, Horton explained all he knew about Luther and the Shipless Pirates.

“Well, Mr. Halfpott, it seems you have saved my life,” she said. “For, I would have died before marrying the pasty cad Luther Luggertuck or, for that matter, any of the idiots in there who tromped all the way down here to try to woo me and my father’s money.”

She stepped out of the bushes and, though I will not dwell on it, Horton felt a gooshing and gushing inside, for—in the light spilling from the ballroom windows—he could see she was directing another wonderful smile at him.

"I have just one concern, though," she said. "When the pirates don't see Little Bo-peep at the ball, they won't give up. Sooner or later they'll find me."

"Oh, no," said Horton, "I hadn't thought of that."

"What we need is a substitute Little Bo-peep," she said.

"Great idea," said Horton, quite impressed. "That would really confuse them."

"Of course," she continued, "the substitute must be someone who can hold his own against pirates. But I don't guess we'll find any brawny footmen who could fit into the dress."

"Actually," said Horton, "I know the perfect person. Twice as tough as any footman and twice as mean as any pirate."

"Will he help us?"

"No," said Horton. "We'll have to trick *her*. She's crafty, but I think I know her weak spot."

40

In Which Miss Neversly's Vanity Is Appealed To . . .

Miss Neversly was, at that moment, in her glory.

Bossing and beating not only her regular kitchen boys, but the footmen and maids whom she'd drafted to help serve the countless platters of food for the guests.

When Celia tapped her on the shoulder, she whipped around, spoon at the ready.

"What is it? Who are you? Why aren't you helping, you young fool?"

“If you please, Miss Neversly,” said Celia, “I’ve been sent from upstairs.”

“Have they run out of cheeses? By the devil’s spatula, I told you cheese boys to move faster! Faster, you drip-nosed pukers!”

“No, ma’am,” interrupted Celia, though she started to doubt that the trick would work. “It’s M’Lady Luggertuck. She wants you to come up!”

Miss Neversly froze.

Celia continued. “M’Lady wants you to come to the ball and take a bow. All the guests want to applaud the cook, she told me.”

Miss Neversly almost fell into a pile of boysenberry custards. Down deep, under the hate and the bile and the meanness, Miss Neversly had always carried a tiny wound. Never in all her years at Smugwick Manor had she ever been thanked by M’Lady Luggertuck. Not for the Cornish hens or the standing rib roasts or the garlic gherkins. Not even for the Luggertuck Breakfast Fruitbraids.

Now, at last, she would get her due. She would be thanked in front of everyone. The spoon dropped from her hand. She began to fuss with her hair.

Celia slipped in the crucial point.

"Ma'am, M'Lady Luggertuck asked that you put a costume on, since everyone else of high importance is wearing a costume."

Celia held up the Little Bo-peep costume. Even now she feared Neversly would refuse.

"It's to distinguish you from the regular servants," Celia added.

As Horton had predicted, Neversly's vanity was stronger than her sense. She grabbed the costume from Celia and began stuffing herself inside. 'Twas a tight fit, but with Celia's help she got it on.

The kitchen staff gaped in dazed disbelief. There stood their boss, their tyrant, their nightmare—dressed in fluffy white skirts and baby-blue bows underneath a puffy cloud of a bonnet. Worst of all, she was smiling. Yes, smiling!

No kitchen boy alive had ever seen that sight before and, later that night in their attic cots, they prayed they never would again. Between her always-chapped lips was a set of teeth that were not the teeth of a human. What they were I cannot say, but when bared in a smile they made one think of the rats that live in deepest basement storerooms under Smugwick.

With a triumphant wave, Miss Neversly floated out the door and up the stairs toward the ballroom, where the gang of Shipless Pirates was waiting for Little Bopeep.

She was hardly in the ballroom for a second when they got her.

The pirates caught her by the cheeses, put a sack over her head, and shuffled her out the door before any of the real guests even noticed her appearance. Not that the guests would have clapped or whistled for her anyway—the leg of lamb was undercooked, the punch tasted watery, and the gherkins smelled too garlicky. Several guests did notice the beautifully polished Luggertuck cutlery, however.

The pirates left by the French doors, then Luther left through the Front Hall, followed at a reasonable distance by Bump, Blight, Blemish, and Portnoy St. Pomfrey, the latter at last fully convinced that Luther was the key to finding the Lump.

41

In Which Luther Proposes . . .

Luther caught up to the pirates at the edge of the mire. (Bump, Blight, Blemish, and St. Pomfrey hid behind the Big Ugly Oak Tree and settled in to watch.)

The pirates had stolen lanterns on their way out of the garden, and these gave enough light for Luther to see their captive. She was still dressed in baby-blue ribbons and frilly white petticoats and still wore the sack over her head.

She fought and clawed and kicked so hard that the crew could barely keep ahold of her.

“All right,” Luther said to the sack. “It’s this simple. Either you agree to marry me or these pirates slit your throat and sink you in the mire.”

The captive squirmed and tried to speak, but the sack muffled her words.

“What’s this?” asked Captain Splinterlock. “You said she was a traitor to the Queen, not some girl who’s broken your barnacled heart!”

“Shut up, what do you care as long as you get paid?”

“Honor is more important than payment, sir,” roared Splinterlock, to the dismay of his crew. “Though I’ll note that we’ve seen no payment yet neither!”

“Here! Here!” Luther shouted, and handed over a large satchel. The pirates all grabbed for it at once.

Luther reached forward and began to undo the turnip sack.

“So, will you marry me or not?”

The sack came off and there, as you know but he didn’t, was Miss Neversly.

“Yes, yes, yes!” she cried. “You didn’t need to go to all this trouble. Of course I’ll marry you!”

42

In Which Things Get Worse and Worse and Worse for Luther . . .

Realizing that he had just proposed to Miss Neversly was the worst thing that had ever happened to Luther Luggertuck.

Seconds later, her acceptance became the new worst thing that had ever happened to him.

And exactly half a second after that, the even newer absolute worst thing was hearing one of the pirates say, "Cap'n, there's no Lump in here!"

"Get me a plank!" roared Captain Splinterlock.

43

In Which a Plank Is Found . . .

"There's nothing here but a bust of Napoleon," snarled patch-eyed Lawrence, who peered into the satchel with disgust.

"Wait!" gasped Luther as Old Bart grabbed him and started squeezing the breath out of him. "The Lump is inside the bust!"

Crash! The bust, which was actually quite valuable, was immediately shattered on the ground. Even in the dim glow of the lanterns, it was clear that there was nothing inside but a crumpled piece of paper.

The patch-eyed man uncrumpled the paper and read aloud: "'Monsieur Smedlap is really Luther Luggertuck, a mean, nasty, rude individual who eats Candied Quail Eggs while his servants eat gruel.'"

Luther was stunned, but the captain wasn't.

"I said, get me a plank!" he bellowed.

"Why, here's a plank right here," cried Lawrence, the patch-eyed pirate.

And lo and behold, there really was a plank.

'Twas old and weathered, but the captain didn't care. He was overjoyed to have a plank again.

"Get ready to walk, Smedlap or Luggertuck or whoever you are," he boomed. "By the beams of my sunken ship, you'll pay for your tricks and your lies! We thought we were catching a traitor, not helping you force yourself on a woman."

"But I want to marry him," cried Miss Neversly, to Luther's horror.

"Irrelevant!" shouted the captain. "No one plays Lose-the-Lump with Captain Obediah Splinterlock! Old Bart, prepare the plank!"

Old Bart laid the plank over a particularly nasty,

deep, muddy section of the mire. Then he shoved Luther toward the end of the plank.

"No, no, I love that man," cried Miss Neversly, to Luther's even greater horror.

Luther's nasty, clever, Luggertuckian brain searched for a new Evil Plan.

"Perhaps," thought Luther, "I could—"

But he was distracted by a nagging thought: Why was there a plank out here in the middle of nowhere? He couldn't imagine why someone would carry a board all the way out here and then leave it, but somehow it seemed familiar . . .

He remembered just as Old Bart gave him a hard kick in the backside. He stumbled forward, teetered for a second on the edge of the plank, and waved his arms in a bid for balance that finally failed.

A disgusting muddy gulp was heard as the mire swallowed him whole.

44

In Which Portnoy St. Pomfrey Finally Gets It Right . . . .

After seeing Luther disappear off the edge of the plank, Bump, Blight, Blemish, and St. Pomfrey left their hiding place and snuck back to the castle. They figured, rightly, that Miss Neversly could take care of herself.

"Egads," whispered St. Pomfrey, pathetically trying to figure out what was happening. "Luther didn't have the Lump after all!"

"Of course not," whispered Bump. "I have it here in my pocket."

"What?" croaked St. Pomfrey.

"Yes, see, here it is," said Bump, and he held up the Lump, which did not glow mysteriously in the moonlight.

St. Pomfrey gazed at it in wonder nonetheless.

"Where was it? How did you know where to find it?"

"Well, sir, I thought about all the things that Luther stole and why," said Bump.

"He stole the wig and the monocle to use as a disguise.

"He stole the stationery to write a letter to the pirates.

"He stole the keys from Old Crotty so that he could sneak around using secret passages, like the one behind Hercules's Armpit. He stole the Lump to pay the kidnappers. But why did he steal the bust of Napoleon and, more importantly, why did he return it?"

A dramatic pause ensued.

"Well," the detective asked impatiently, "why?"

"Why, to hide the Lump in, of course. Once you—the most famous detective in England arrived—he couldn't risk keeping the Lump in his own room or on his person, but he still needed to keep it handy.

"So, he stole the bust, hollowed it out, and stuffed the Lump inside.

"Then he hid it right above our noses on the mantel

in the Front Hall, so that tonight when the kidnappers got Little Bo-peep, he could grab it quickly on his way out the door."

St. Pomfrey interrupted.

"Yes, yes, we just saw him take Napoleon off the mantel. But why wasn't the Lump inside it?"

"Because," said Bump, "Blemish, Blight, and I had already visited Napoleon this afternoon and removed the Lump and inserted that note."

And with that, he handed the Lump to the wide-eyed detective.

Bump, Blight, and Blemish shook hands to celebrate a job well done.

St. Pomfrey stared vacantly at the Lump for several minutes.

Finally, he said, "You boys are pretty good detectives. How would you like jobs with my detective agency in London?"

"Really?" cried all three boys at once.

"Absolutely!" said the detective, who knew the boys would work cheap.

"It does not, I hope, involve the shoveling of manure, does it?" asked Blemish.

“No, my boy, in fact I shall have to insist that none of you spend any more time around manure. You will be sleuthing for sultans, traveling to distant vistas, guesting in overdecorated English manors, and eating as much of your clients’ food as you can eat. The smell of dung simply will not fit in.”

This sounded mighty good to the boys. Pretty close to a dream come true. Of course they accepted St. Pomfrey’s offer.

“Fine, it’s all settled then,” said St. Pomfrey. “Of course, as employees of St. Pomfrey Detection, Inc., your share of the Lump reward naturally goes to the company treasury.”

(Reader, you will not be surprised to learn that the company treasury and St. Pomfrey’s personal bank account were one and the same.)

But Bump, Blight, and Blemish didn’t care. They were getting out of the stables at last.

“And I’m sure you’ll also understand that—for the good of the company—people must believe that I, Portnoy St. Pomfrey, the greatest detective in all of England, solved the case. I regret that I must take all the credit when we return to the manor, but I must. I must.”

45

In Which M'Lady Luggertuck Almost Gets Her Lump Back . . .

St. Pomfrey, with the stable boys close behind, made a grand entrance back at the costume ball, just as the clock struck midnight.

"M'Lady Luggertuck, I bring you the Lump, stolen by your own son and rescued by me from his murderers at enormous risk to myself and my associates, requiring the doubling of my fee," he pronounced grandiloquently, ostentatiously, and falsely.

He presented the Lump with a grand flourish.

Unfortunately, his fingers, damp from his evening in the mire, lost their grip on the heavy stone as he flourished. The Lump slipped away and sailed through the air.

M'Lady Luggertuck, overlooking the news that her son had been murdered, screamed, "My Lump!"

The assembled guests gasped. The musicians stopped playing, all except a tuba player whose instrument let out a long *"bluuuuuuug."*

The Lump's graceful arc ended with a dull thud on the polished ballroom floor. It made a morose tinkle as it shattered into a hundred pieces of ordinary rock. It was not and had never been the world's biggest uncut diamond.

The pride of ten generations of Luggertucks was worthless.

M'Lady fainted. Sir Luggertuck fainted. Crotty fainted. The colonel, who had been dozing in a chair, woke up, was told what had happened, and then fainted.

Gateberry, Howbag, and Hillhemp—peeking through a window—realized that they were witnessing the greatest story of their careers and fainted.

Faintings, Reader, are not all created equal. The

colonel's faint, for example, was just a little flop. Crotty's was a crumple.

M'Lady Luggertuck's faint 'twas neither a little flop nor a crumple—'twas the toppling of a titan, already top heavy because of her monstrous wig. Guests ran for safety as she teetered first one way, then the next.

Reader, I fear I must pause here before M'Lady falls to discuss Miss Neversly's Pickle Éclairs. They were pale green and gross and, since not a single one had been sampled by a guest, they were still piled high on a platter that sat at one end of the pickle table.

I needed to tell you that because when M'Lady Luggertuck fainted, it was upon the opposite end of the aforementioned pickle table that she landed with all the force of a felled tree.

That caused the éclair end of the aforementioned pickle table to rise suddenly. Which led, inevitably, to the platter of Miss Neversly's Pickle Éclairs being launched high into the air.

Up, up, up they soared—almost touching the dazzling chandelier—before gravity returned them speedily down, down, down to earth.

Thwack, thwack, thwack. They rained down upon the

guests, who desperately sought shelter under chairs, credenzas, and servants.

I'm not sorry to say that the final éclair landed with a particularly loud *thwack* right in the middle of M'Lady Luggertuck's forehead, dislodging her wig and revealing her gray hair for all to see. It was a mercy, really, that she was unconscious.

Lord Emberly, who had come to the ball only to get some of Loafburton's Royal Rum Plum Rumpus, laughed and laughed until tears ran down his whiskers.

46

In Which M'Lady Goes to Bed Early . . .

Crotty was revived by the adoring Footman Jennings. Together they helped M'Lady Luggertuck back to her room. She did not return to the ball.

The new maid, Milly, now painfully aware of what life at Smugwick Manor was really like, grudgingly slunk forward with a mop and bucket to clean up the soggy clumps of green éclair.

"Allow me to help," came a kindly voice. Well, Lord-Love-a-Duck! It was Montgomery!

He took the mop from Milly, who smiled and blushed

and batted her eyelashes. (Reader, I'm as flabbergasted as you are! Love really did bloom for Montgomery after all. Who would have guessed it?)

The musicians began to play again, although they were nearly drowned out by all the guests gossiping about the Luggertucks' humiliation. This would be the talk of the season.

Horton and Celia, who had watched the whole thing through the French doors, entered the ballroom to talk to Bump, Blight, and Blemish. Horton was dying to find out where the Lump had been hidden. Bump was dying to find out how Miss Neversly came to be dressed as Little Bo-peep.

They supplied each other with the pertinent facts, while everyone, including Horton, ate several helpings of Sweet Sugarapple Pie. Bump, Blight, and Blemish went off to ring the purple bell, so that all the servants could join what had surprisingly turned out to be a very nice evening at Smugwick Manor.

47

In Which Two Young People Finally Get a Moment of Peace in Which to Speak Pleasantly to Each Other . . .

Celia introduced Horton to the Shortleys, who quite liked him and said they would be delighted to have him as their guest for the rest of the summer.

"Why, you may as well ride back with us in the carriage this very night," suggested Mrs. Shortley.

That wouldn't be proper, Horton knew, and he was about to say so when Mr. Shortley started talking.

"By the way, young Halfpott," said Mr. Shortley. "I

was very sorry to hear from Celia about your father's poor health. He and I were at school together, you know. I asked my personal physician to drop round and see him. The doctor confided to me that he has begun a promising treatment of medicines and hopes to see a rapid improvement."

Horton, both grateful and confused, barely had time to say thank you before the Shortleys waltzed away to join in the latest dance.

"Would you like to dance, Horton?" asked Celia.

She was beaming, but Horton felt terrible. He felt he had misled Celia and the Shortleys. He knew it was time to say what should have been said long ago.

"Er, don't you realize that I can't dance with you? And I can't stay with the Shortleys? I'm just a servant. A kitchen boy. I shouldn't even be talking to you."

"But that's not true," Celia protested.

"Yes," argued Horton. "Yes, I am."

"No, Horton," said Celia, laughing. "I don't think you really are a kitchen boy anymore. Or at least you won't be tomorrow morning when M'Lady Luggertuck wakes up and figures out what happened. I seriously doubt she'll want you working in her kitchen after this."

(This turned out to be an understatement of enormous magnitude.)

"And anyway, I don't care if you work in a kitchen or not," said Celia. "You're a friend of mine and that's all that matters."

And lo and behold, Reader, she kissed him.

Now, she meant to just kiss him on the cheek, but by some little accident her lips went astray and landed upon his. Please, may we dwell on that for just a moment? It was the first kiss she ever gave and the first he ever got and neither one of them ever forgot exactly what it felt like.

Then they danced—or at least Horton attempted to. He wasn't doing well to start with and then he stepped in one of the splattered éclairs.

But no matter! They laughed and talked and—yes, I will say it—kissed again.

Horton was very, very happy and that is the last and best Unprecedented Marvel of our story.

48

In Which M'Lady Luggertuck Gives Crotty Instructions Regarding Her Corset . . .

The next morning, M'Lady Luggertuck awoke to learn that her son, Luther, was not dead. He had been found half-drowned, humiliated, and thoroughly covered in stinking, putrid mire mud. The footmen were giving him a good scrub in the horse trough, Crotty told her.

The Lump, however, was still as worthless as it had been last night.

M'Lady Luggertuck showed no emotion at either of

these facts. She sat wordlessly as Crotty dressed her.

Finally, as Crotty put the corset on, she spoke: "Tighter, Crotty, tighter."

Acknowledgments

Charles Dickens inspired this story. Cece Bell and Robbie Mayes helped me write it. Caryn Wiseman found a home for it. Susan Van Metre believed in it and knew how to make it better. Gilbert Ford, Chad W. Beckerman, and Melissa Arnst made it beautiful. Jason Wells and Laura Mihalick figured out how to tell everybody about it.

From there, librarians, teachers, booksellers, and bloggers endeavoured to put it into your hands.

I thank all of them and I thank you, dear Reader, for opening it.

Tom Angleberger once worked as a kitchen boy—forced to grease potatoes, spoon up cobblers, and make forty pounds of coleslaw a night for a big restaurant. He later worked with the real Hillhemp, Howbag, and Gateberry at a newspaper. But now he writes books, including *The Strange Case of Origami Yoda*.

Many authors helped inspire Tom to write the story of Horton Halfpott, and you may find some of their names in the book, if you look carefully enough. Most important were Charles Dickens, who is funnier than you would think, and Daniel Pinkwater, who is funnier than a pickle éclair. Tom lives in Virginia, and he hopes, dear Reader, that you will visit him online at www.hortonhalfpott.com.

This book was designed by Melissa Arnst and art directed by Chad W. Beckerman. The text is set in 11.5-point Baskerville, a font designed in 1757 by John Baskerville, an English typographer and printer. Somewhat dissatisfied with the heavy popular type styles of the time, he created his own distinct style, which was more delicate. He examined various faces for their ease of reading, and found that finer types were easier to read, especially when printed in the smaller sizes used in books. Baskerville's type style is appreciated today as one of the best choices for printed books. The display font is Tree-Monkey Puzzle.

SNOOPING STABLEBOYS

M'LADY LUGGERTUCK

CONSTABLE WHOLECLOTH

NEVERFSLY V. LOAFBURTON

SIR FALSTAFF

COL. SITWELL

SWALLOWED BY THE MIRE

BUMP IN
THE DARK

NAPOLEON

LORD EMBERLY

HILLHEMP, HEGBAG, GATEBERRY

OLD BART

THE DISHES

SIEGFRIED

BLIGHT + BLEMISH

LUTHER AND MONTGOMERY
THE LUMP
CELIA
SMUGWICK MANOR
MONSIEUR SMEDLAP
THE PERFUMING
HORTON
THE ABDUCTION!!
PORTNOY SLEEPS
OLD CROTTY
MERVYN
THE SUITORS